"So why did you want to see me?"

Tamsin's pulse faltered. She shot to her feet and stepped away, needing distance. "It's about the archives I'm cataloging and assessing for conservation."

She turned. Alaric stood by the chair, frowning in abstraction. Tamsin lifted her chin, breathing deeply.

"One of the documents caught my attention. It's a record of your family. There's still work to be done on it." Tamsin paused, keeping her voice even. "I've been translating from the Latin, and if it's proved correct…"

"Yes? If it's proved correct…?"

Tamsin hesitated, but there was no easy way to say it.

"If it's genuine you're not only Prince of Ruvingia, you're also the next legitimate ruler of the whole country." She paused, watching his expression freeze. "It's you who should be crowned king."

ANNIE WEST discovered romance early—her childhood best friend's house was an unending store of Harlequin books—and she's been addicted ever since. Fortunately she found her own real-life romantic hero while studying at university, and she married him. After gaining (despite the distraction) an honors classics degree, Annie took a job in the public service. For years she wrote and redrafted and revised—government plans, letters for cabinet ministers and reports for parliament. Checking the text of a novel is so much more fun!

Annie started to write romance when she took leave to spend time with her children. Between school activities she produced her first novel. At the same time she discovered Romance Writers of Australia. Since then she's been active in RWAus writers' groups and competitions. She attends annual conferences and loves the support she gets from so many other writers. Her first Harlequin novel came out in 2005.

Annie lives with her hero (still the same one) and her children at Lake Macquarie, north of Sydney, and spends her time fantasizing about gorgeous men and their love lives. It's hard work, but she has no regrets!

Annie loves to hear from readers. You can contact her via her website, www.annie-west.com, or at annie@annie-west.com.

PROTECTED BY THE PRINCE

ANNIE WEST

~ THE WEIGHT OF THE CROWN ~

TORONTO • NEW YORK • LONDON
AMSTERDAM • PARIS • SYDNEY • HAMBURG
STOCKHOLM • ATHENS • TOKYO • MILAN • MADRID
PRAGUE • WARSAW • BUDAPEST • AUCKLAND

Recycling programs
for this product may
not exist in your area.

ISBN-13: 978-0-373-52801-1

PROTECTED BY THE PRINCE

Previously published in the U.K. under the title
PASSION, PURITY AND THE PRINCE

First North American Publication 2011

Printed in U.S.A.

PROTECTED BY
THE PRINCE

For Dorothy and Len, my wonderful parents.
With thanks and love always.

CHAPTER ONE

'HIS HIGHNESS will be here soon. Please remain in this room and *do not wander*. There are strict security controls and alarms in this part of the castle.'

The prince's aide spoke in clipped English and gave Tamsin a stern look. As if after finally passing the barriers of royal protocol and officious secretaries she'd run amok now she was within the royal sanctum.

As if, after weeks working in the Ruvingian royal archives and living in her suite on the far side of the castle courtyard, proximity to flesh and blood royalty might be too much for her! She'd never seen the prince. He never deigned to cross the courtyard to the functional archive room.

She stifled an impatient sigh.

Did she look the sort of woman to be overcome by pomp and wealth? Or be impressed by a man whose reputation as a womaniser and adventurer rivalled even that of his infamous robber baron ancestors?

Tamsin had more important things on her mind.

Secret excitement rippled through her and it had nothing to do with meeting a playboy prince.

This was her chance to rebuild her reputation. After Patrick's brutal betrayal she could finally prove herself to her colleagues and herself. Her confidence had shattered after the way he'd used her. He'd damaged her professionally but far worse, he'd hurt her so badly she'd wanted only to crawl away and lick her wounds.

She'd never trust again.

Some scars wouldn't heal. Yet here, now, she could at least kick start her career again. This was a once in a lifetime opportunity and she was ready for the challenge.

For ten days Prince Alaric had been too busy to meet her. His schedule had been too full to fit her in. Clearly an expert on old books didn't rank in his priorities.

The notion ignited a shimmer of anger inside her. She was tired of being used, dismissed and overlooked.

Had he hoped to fob her off by seeing her so late in the evening? Tamsin straightened her spine, clasping her hands in her lap, ankles crossed demurely under the massive chair.

'Of course I won't leave. I'll be content here until His Highness arrives.'

The aide's dubious expression made it clear he thought she was waiting her moment to sneak off and gape at the VIPs in the ballroom. Or maybe steal the silverware.

Impatient at the way he hovered, she slipped a hand into her briefcase and pulled out a wad of papers. She gave the aide a perfunctory smile and started reading.

'Very well.' His voice interrupted and she looked up. 'It's possible the prince may be...delayed. If you need anything, ring the bell.'

He gestured to a switch on the wall, camouflaged by the exquisite wood carving surrounding the huge fireplace. 'Refreshments will be brought if you need them.'

'Thank you.' Tamsin nodded and watched him bustle away.

Was 'delay' code? Was the prince busy seducing a glamorous beauty from the ball? If gossip was right Prince Alaric of Ruvingia, in line to the crown of Maritz, was a playboy *par excellence*. Pursuing women would be higher on his priorities than meeting a book curator.

Tamsin ignored a fizz of indignation.

Her gaze strayed to the ceiling height bookshelves. The inevitable spark of interest quickened her blood. Old books. She smelled the familiar scent of aged paper and leather.

If he was going to be late...

Not allowing herself second thoughts, Tamsin walked to the nearest bookcase. It was too much to hope it would yield anything as exciting as what she'd unearthed in the archives, but why sit reading documents she knew by heart?

Her reluctant host was probably hours away.

* * *

'You must excuse me, Katarina. I have business to attend to.' Alaric disengaged himself from the countess's clinging grasp.

'So late? Surely there are better ways to spend the night?' Her ruby lips parted and her silvery eyes flashed a familiar message. Sexual promise, excitement and just a touch of greed. She swayed forward, her barely covered breasts straining against her ball gown, her emerald-strewn cleavage designed to draw the eye.

Acquiring lovers had always been easy for Alaric but he was tired of being targeted by women like Katarina.

His rules were simple. First, no long term commitment. Ever. Emotional intimacy, what others called love, was a mirage he knew to be dangerous and false. Second, he did the chasing.

He needed diversion but on *his* terms.

Katarina, despite her genuine sexual desire, was another who'd set her sights on marriage. Permanency. Royal prestige. Wealth. Right now he had more significant concerns than satisfying the ambitions of a grasping socialite.

'Sadly it's a meeting I can't avoid.' Over her head he caught the eye of the steward hovering at the entrance. 'Your car is here.' He lifted her hand, barely brushing it with his lips, before leading her to the door.

'I'll call you,' she whispered, her voice sultry.

Alaric smiled easily, secure in the knowledge she wouldn't get past his staff.

Five minutes later, with the last guests gone, he dismissed his personal staff and strode down the corridor, his mind returning to the recent conversation with Raul.

If anyone else had asked him to stay here, cooped up through winter, Alaric would have ignored them. The need to be out and doing something, keeping busy, was a turbulent tide rising in his blood. The idea of six more months tied to his alpine principality gave him cabin fever.

It might be home, but he felt hemmed in. Constricted. Prey to the darkness clawing from within.

Only constant action and diversion kept him from succumbing. Kept him sane.

Alaric forked a hand through his hair, impatiently flicking his cape off one shoulder. That was another thing to thank his distant cousin and soon-to-be monarch for. An evening wearing the outmoded uniform of two centuries ago.

Yet he'd given his word. He must help Raul.

After decades of peace, the recent death of the old king, Raul's father, had reignited unrest. Alaric's principality of Ruvingia was stable but elsewhere tensions that had almost led to civil war a generation ago had reopened. With careful management danger would be averted, but they couldn't take chances.

He and Raul had to ensure stability. In their nation of Maritz, clinging to monarchical traditions, that meant a calm, united front in the lead up to his cousin's coronation and the reopening of parliament.

So here Alaric was, cutting ribbons and hosting balls!

He swung into another corridor, itching for action. But this wasn't as simple as leading a commando squad to disarm combatants. There was no violence. Yet.

Alaric's belly twisted as the ghosts of the past stirred, a reminder of how suddenly tragedy could strike.

With an effort he shoved aside the lingering pain and glanced at his watch. He was miles late for his last obligation of the day. As soon as it was over he'd escape for a few hours. Take the Aston Martin over the mountain pass and try out its paces on the hairpin bends.

Alaric quickened his step at the beckoning sense of freedom, however temporary.

Another twist in the ancient passage and there was the library door. Automatically he slowed, acknowledging but not yielding to the frisson of discomfort feathering his spine.

This would never be his study, no matter what the staff expected. It was his father's room, his brother's. Alaric preferred the mobility of a laptop he could use elsewhere. Preferred not to be reminded he walked in dead men's shoes.

Too many dead men.

Fragmented images rose. At the forefront was Felix, his talented, capable, older brother.

The one who should be here instead of Alaric.

Who'd died because of Alaric.

The frisson of awareness froze into a gut-stabbing shaft of ice. Familiar guilt engulfed him. Pain tore his chest and throat with each breath.

He accepted it as inevitable. *His punishment.* The weight he would always bear.

Eventually he forced his breathing to slow and his legs to move.

The room was empty. Logs burned in the fireplace, lamps glowed but no expert waited to harangue him about the state of the archives. If the matter was so urgent surely she'd have stayed.

All the better. He could be on the open road in ten minutes.

He was turning away when a stack of papers caught his attention. A battered briefcase sagged on the floor. Immediately he was alert, his gaze narrowing.

Then he heard it, an almost imperceptible swish from above. Instincts honed on the edge of survival sharpened. He flexed his fingers. An instant later, hand on the hilt of his ceremonial sword, he faced the intruder.

For long moments he stared, then his hand fell away.

The room had been invaded by a…mushroom.

On top of the ladder fixed to the bookshelves perched a shapeless muddle of grey-brown. A long granny cardigan the colour of dust caught his eye and beneath, spread across the ladder top that now served as a seat, a voluminous grey skirt. It was a woman, though her clothes looked like something that had sprouted on a damp forest floor.

A wall sconce shone on dark hair, scraped back, and a glint of glasses above a massive book. White-gloved hands held the volume up, obscuring her face. And beneath…his gaze riveted on the rhythmic swing of a leg, bare to just above the knee.

One seriously sexy leg.

Alaric paced closer, his attention gratefully diverted from sombre remembrances.

Skin like moonlight. A shapely calf, trim ankle and neat foot. Toes that wriggled enticingly with each swing.

Masculine appreciation stirred as his gaze slid back up her leg. Even her knee looked good! Too good to be teasing a man who was restless and in desperate need of distraction.

He crossed to the base of the ladder and picked up a discarded shoe. Flat soled, plain brown, narrow and neat. Appallingly dowdy.

He raised his brows. Those legs deserved something better, assuming the one tucked beneath that horror of a skirt matched the elegant limb on show. They demanded heels. Stiletto sharp and high, to emphasise the luscious curve of her calf. Ankle straps. Ribbons, sexy enough to tease a man till he took them off and moved on to other pleasures.

Alaric shook his head. He'd bet all the jewels in the basement vault the owner of this shoe would be horrified at the extravagance of footwear designed to seduce a man.

A tingle of something dangerously like anticipation feathered his neck as he watched her leg swing and her foot arch seductively. This time the little wriggle of her toes seemed deliciously abandoned as if the drab clothes camouflaged a secret sybarite.

Alaric's mood lightened for the first time in weeks.

'Cinderella, I presume?'

The voice was deep and mellow, jolting Tamsin out of her reverie. Warily she lowered the volume enough to peer over it.

She froze, eyes widening as she took in the man gazing up at her.

He'd stepped out of a fantasy.

He couldn't be real. No flesh and blood man looked like that. So mouth-wateringly wonderful.

Numb with shock, she shook her head in automatic disbelief. He could have been Prince Charming, standing there in his elaborate hussar's uniform, her discarded shoe in one large, capable hand. A bigger, tougher Prince Charming than she remembered from her childhood reading. His dark eyebrows slashed across a tanned face that wasn't so much handsome as magnetic, charismatic, potently sexy.

Like Prince Charming's far more experienced and infinitely more dangerous older brother.

Eyes, dark and gleaming, transfixed her. They were... aware.

Meeting his unblinking regard she had the crazy notion that for the first time ever a man looked and really saw *her*. Not her reputation, not her misfit status but the real flesh and blood Tamsin Connors, the impulsive woman she'd tried so hard to stifle.

She felt vulnerable, yet thrilled.

A lazy smile lifted one corner of his mouth and a deep groove creased his cheek.

Stunned, she felt a squiggle of response deep in her abdomen. Tiny rivers of fire quivered under her skin. Her lungs squeezed her breath out in a whoosh of...of...

The book she held shut with a snap that made her jump. Instantly the other volumes in her lap slid and she grabbed for them. But they were cumbersome and she didn't dare let go of the precious herbal in her hands.

In dry mouthed horror she watched a book tumble out of her grasp. It fell in slow motion, turning over as it went. Even knowing it was too late to save the volume she scrabbled for it, barely keeping her precarious perch.

'Don't move!' The authority in his voice stopped her in mid lunge.

He strode forward a step, stretched out his hand and the book fell into his grasp as if it belonged there.

Dizzy with relief, Tamsin shut her eyes. She'd never have forgiven herself if it had been damaged.

How had he done that? The volume was no paperback. It weighed a ton. Yet he'd caught it one-handed from a fall of twelve feet as if it were feather light.

Tamsin snapped her eyes open and saw him turn to place the book on the desk. The indigo material of his tunic clung to his broad shoulder and muscled arm.

That formidable figure wasn't the result of tailored padding.

She swallowed hard, her gaze dropping to long powerful thighs encased in dark trousers. The crimson stripe down the side drew attention to the strength of those limbs.

No pretend soldier. The straight set of his shoulders and the contained power of each precise movement proclaimed him the real thing.

Abruptly he turned, as if sensing her scrutiny. His gaze pierced her and she shivered, overwhelmingly aware of him as *male*.

She worked with men all the time, but she'd never met one so undeniably masculine. As if testosterone radiated off him in waves. It made her heart race.

'Now to get you safely down.' Was that a glint of humour in his eyes?

'I'm OK.' She clutched the books like a lifeline. 'I'll put these back and—'

'No.' The single syllable stopped her. 'I'll take them.'

'I promise you I'm not usually so clumsy.' She sat straighter, annoyed at her stupidity in examining the books here instead of taking them to the desk. Normally she was methodical, logical and careful. It was no excuse that excitement had overridden her caution.

'Nevertheless, it's not worth the risk.' He walked to the foot of the ladder and looked up, his face unreadable. 'I'll relieve you of your burden first.'

Tamsin bit her lip. She couldn't blame him. She'd almost damaged a unique volume. What sort of expert took such risks? What she'd done was unforgivable.

'I'm sorry, I—'

Her words cut out as the ladder moved beneath her, a rhythmic sway as he nimbly closed the distance between them.

Tamsin became excruciatingly self-aware as his ascent slowed. Warm breath feathered her bare ankle then shivered against her calf and to her horror she couldn't repress a delicious little shudder.

A moment later a dark head appeared in the V between her splayed knees. Something hard and hot plunged down through her abdomen as she met his gaze.

From metres away this man was stunning. Up close, where she could see the twinkle lurking in midnight-blue eyes and the sensuous curve of his full lower lip, he stole her breath. Tiny lines beside his mouth and eyes spoke of experience and a grim endurance at odds with his easy humour. Yet they only accentuated his attractiveness.

Her heart beat a rapid tattoo that pulsed adrenaline through her body and robbed her of coherent thought.

'Allow me.' Large hands reached out and scooped the book from her lap, barely ruffling her skirt. Yet his heat seared through her clothing and suddenly she felt dizzy. She clutched the herbal to her breast.

Then he was gone, swarming down the ladder with an ease that spoke of supreme fitness and agility.

Tamsin drew a deep breath into constricted lungs, searching for composure. She'd never been distracted by male beauty before. She dismissed as irrelevant the knowledge that she'd never seen anyone so magnificent.

She shook her head. He's just a man, just—

'This one, too.' There he was again. She'd been so caught up in her thoughts she hadn't noticed his rapid ascent. He reached for the book in her arms.

'It's all right. I can carry it.' For suddenly, close enough to inhale his subtle spice and forest and man scent, she didn't want to relinquish the barrier between them. She clung to it like a talisman.

'We don't want to risk another accident,' he drawled in his easy, perfect English. 'Do we, Cinderella?'

'I'm not...' She stopped herself. Despite his mock serious expression there was amusement in his eyes.

Anger welled. Self-consciousness tightened her stomach. Patrick laughed at her too. All her life she'd been a misfit, a figure of speculation and amusement. She'd learned to pretend not to notice but still it hurt.

Yet this was her fault. She'd put herself in this ridiculous position because she'd been too curious to sit meekly waiting. She'd never be taken seriously now. Just when it was vital she win confidence and trust.

Had she single-handedly wrecked her chance of success?

Summoning the scraps of her dignity she unclamped stiff fingers and lowered the volume into his waiting hands.

Calloused fingers brushed hers through the thin gloves she'd donned to protect the books. An electric shock shot up her arm and across her breasts. She jerked her hands away.

Tamsin bit the inside of her cheek and looked away from his knowing gaze, her emotions too raw for comfort.

He stood still. She felt his stare, tangible as a trailing touch, move across her face to her throat then back up again. Her breathing shallowed.

She told herself she was used to being a curiosity, out of step with her peers. Stubbornly she ignored the hurt lancing her chest.

An instant later he clattered back down the ladder and she let out her breath in a sigh.

Time to climb down and face the music. She unfolded the leg tucked beneath her. Pins and needles prickled, proof she'd sat here longer than she'd realised. Gingerly she wriggled, pulling the bunched hem of her skirt down where it had rucked up. Grasping the ladder she rose, ready to turn.

His appearance before her prevented her moving.

'I need space to turn around.' Her voice was betrayingly uneven.

Instead of descending, he rose, his hands grasping the top of the ladder so his broad shoulders and powerful arms surrounded her.

Something fluttered in Tamsin's chest at the sensation of being caught within his embrace, though he didn't touch her. The force field of his presence engulfed her. It made her feel small and vulnerable and edgy.

Her breath hissed in.

His head was at breast height now. She leaned back towards the shelving, trying to put space between them.

'Whoa. Easy now.' His deep voice lowered to a soothing pitch, as if steadying a fractious animal.

'I can climb down alone.' Her words were sharper than she'd intended, betraying her embarrassment at the storm of inexplicable reactions bombarding her.

'Of course you can.' His lips pursed ruminatively, drawing her eyes. Heat washed her neck and cheeks as she stared. In a less rugged face that perfect mouth would look almost feminine. But on him those lips simply looked sensuous and dangerously inviting.

Like the deeply hooded eyes that steadily surveyed her.

Tamsin swallowed and felt her blush burn hotter. Could he read her thoughts? He must be accustomed to women gaping. The realisation didn't ease her embarrassment.

'But accidents happen and I wouldn't want you losing your footing.'

'I won't lose my footing,' she said in a horribly breathless voice.

He shrugged those wide, straight shoulders, mesmerising her with the movement. 'We hope not. But we won't take chances. Think of the insurance claim if you're injured.'

'I wouldn't—'

'Of course you wouldn't.' He rose further and she backed so her shoulders touched the bookshelf and there was nowhere else to go. 'But your permanent employer might sue for damages if you're injured due to our negligence.'

'It's not your negligence. I climbed up here.'

He shook his head. 'Anyone with an ounce of understanding would realise what temptation this ladder is to a woman who loves books. It's asking for trouble.'

Something flickered in his eyes. She was sure he was laughing but his sympathetic expression couldn't be faulted. 'It was irresponsible to leave it here, just begging to be climbed.'

He conveniently ignored the fact that the ladder was fixed top and bottom to the rails placed around the walls.

'You're talking nonsense.'

His eyebrows arched and a flash of something that might have been approval lit his eyes.

'Very probably,' he murmured. 'The tension must be getting to me. Heights can affect people like that, you know.' His lips curved up in another one of those half-smiles that melted something vital inside her. 'Take pity on my nerves and let me get you down from here.'

Tamsin opened her mouth to end his games. She refused to be the butt of his jokes. But before she could speak large hands pulled her towards him, warming her through several layers of clothing and jamming the words in her throat. For a moment panic threatened as she plunged forward, but an instant later she was draped over one solid shoulder. He clamped her close with his arm and then he was moving, descending the ladder with her firmly in his hold.

'Put me down! Let me go, *right now!*' She couldn't believe he'd grabbed her.

'Of course. In just a moment.'

To her horror Tamsin *felt* his deep voice rumble through his torso and hers.

Tamsin shut her eyes rather than look at the distant floor, or, more disturbingly, the intriguing sight of muscles bunching in the taut backside inches from her face.

But closing her eyes heightened other senses. She felt him against the length of her body, his strength undeniably exciting as ripples of movement teased her breasts and thighs. Disturbing warmth swirled languidly in the pit of her stomach.

She shouldn't be enjoying this. She should be outraged. Or at least impervious. She should…

'There.' He lowered her into a chair and stepped back. 'Safe and sound.'

His eyes weren't laughing now. They were sober as he stared down at her. His mouth was a firm line, his brows tipped into a slight frown as if the joke had turned sour. His jaw clamped hard and she had the fleeting impression he was annoyed rather than amused.

Tamsin wanted desperately to conjure a witty quip. To redeem herself as clever and insouciant, taking the situation in her stride.

Instead she gazed helplessly, enmeshed in a web of unfamiliar reactions. Her breasts tingled from contact with him, her nipples puckering shamelessly. Her thighs were warm from his touch. Her gaze caught on his black hair, now slightly rumpled. Heat sizzled inside like a firecracker about to explode.

It wasn't the sexy cavalry uniform that made him look so good, despite the gilt braiding that moulded his tapering torso, the cut of clothes that made him look every inch the fairy tale hero. What unnerved her was the flesh and blood man whose shadowed eyes glowed like an invitation to sin.

She tried to tell herself he was vain enough to have a uniform designed to enhance the incredible colour of his eyes. But the gravity of his expression when he wasn't smiling told her he didn't give a toss for his looks.

Tamsin's breath sawed as he dropped to one knee and took her bare foot in his hand. Tremors rippled up her leg and she felt again that strange molten sensation pooling low in her belly.

She squirmed but he didn't release her. Instead he fished something out of his pocket and slid it onto her foot. Soft, worn familiar leather. Her discarded shoe.

'So, Cinderella. Why did you want to see me?'

Tamsin's pulse faltered. For the last ten minutes she'd pretended he was a guest, even a member of staff. Yet deep inside she'd known who he was.

Prince Alaric. The man who held her career and her reputation in his hands.

Already she amused him. How he'd laugh if he knew that in ten minutes, without trying, he'd seduced one of Britain's last dyed in the wool virgins to mindless longing.

Tamsin swallowed convulsively. She shot to her feet and stepped away, busying herself by stripping off her gloves and stuffing them in a pocket.

'It's about the archives I'm cataloguing and assessing for conservation.' A cache of documents recently discovered when a castle cellar had been remodelled.

She turned. He stood by the chair, frowning in abstraction. Tamsin lifted her chin, breathing deep.

'They include some unique and valuable papers.'

'I'm sure they do.' He nodded, his expression blandly polite. Obviously he had no interest in her efforts.

'I have a copy of one with me.' She reached for her briefcase, grateful for an excuse to look away from his hooded gaze.

'Why don't you just tell me about it?'

Cut to the chase, in other words.

He'd had plenty of time to dally, amusing himself at her expense, but none to spare for her work.

Disappointment curled through her, and annoyance.

'One of the documents caught my attention. It's a record of your family and Prince Raul's.' She paused, excitement at her find bubbling up despite her vexation.

'There's still work to be done on it.' Tamsin paused, keeping her voice carefully even. 'I've been translating from the Latin and, if it's proved correct…'

'Yes? If it's proved correct?'

Tamsin hesitated, but there was no easy way to say it. Besides, he'd surely welcome the news.

'If it's genuine you're not only Prince of Ruvingia, you're also the next legitimate ruler of Maritz. Of the whole country. Not Prince Raul.' She paused, watching his expression freeze.

'It's you who should be crowned king.'

CHAPTER TWO

ALARIC'S body stiffened as her words sank in with terrible, nightmare clarity.

Him as ruler of Maritz!

The idea was appalling.

Raul was the crown prince. The one brought up from birth to rule. The one trained and ready to dedicate his life to his country.

Maritz needed him.

Or a man like Alaric's brother, Felix.

Alaric wasn't in the same mould. Even now he heard his father's cool, clipped voice expressing endless displeasure and disappointment with his reckless second son.

Alaric's lips twisted. How right the old man had been. Alaric couldn't take responsibility for the country. Bad enough he'd stepped into Felix's shoes as leader of a principality. Entrusting the wellbeing of the whole nation to his keeping would be disaster.

He, whose conscience was heavy with the weight of others' lives! Who'd failed them so abysmally.

Horror crawled up his spine to clamp his shoulders. Ice froze his blood. Familiar faces swam in his vision, faces distorted with pain. The faces of those he'd failed. The face of his brother, eyes feverish as he berated Alaric for betraying him.

He couldn't be king. It was unthinkable.

'Is this a joke?' The words shot out, harsh in the silence.

'Of course not!'

No. One look at her frown and her stunned eyes made that clear. Tamsin Connors wasn't kidding.

He'd never seen a more serious, buttoned-up woman. From her tense lips to her heavy-framed glasses and scraped-back hair, she was the image of no-nonsense spinsterhood.

Except for that body.

Hard to believe she'd felt so warm and lithely curved. Or that holding her he'd known a curious desire to strip away that fashion crime of an outfit and explore her scented femininity. A desire completely dormant in the face of so many blatant sexual invitations from tonight's beauties!

Beneath her bag lady clothes Tamsin Connors was only in her mid-twenties. When she forgot to prim them her lips were surprisingly luscious. He looked into her frowning face and knew he was avoiding the issue. The impossible issue of him being king!

'What exactly is in these papers?' His voice sounded rusty, as if his vocal cords had seized up.

'They're old records by a cleric called Tomas. He detailed royal history, especially births, deaths and marriages.' She shifted, leaning imperceptibly closer.

Did he imagine her fresh sunshine scent, warm in a room chilled with the remembrance of death?

With an effort he dragged his focus back to her.

'Take a seat, please, and explain.' He gestured to one of the armchairs by the fire then took one for himself.

'According to Tomas there was intermarriage between your family and Prince Raul's.'

Alaric nodded. 'That was common practice.' Power was guarded through alliances with other aristocratic families.

'At one stage there was a gap in the direct line to the Maritzian throne. The crown couldn't pass from father to son as the king's son had died.'

Her words flayed a raw spot deep inside him. A familiar glacial chill burned Alaric's gut. The knowledge he was a usurper in a better man's shoes.

That he was responsible for his brother's death.

'There were two contenders for the throne. One from Prince Raul's family and…' Her words slowed as she registered his expression. Some of her enthusiasm faded.

'And one from mine?'

She shifted as if uncomfortable, but continued.

Two rival princes from different branches of intertwined families. A will from the old king designating one, the eldest by some weeks, as his successor. A tragic 'accident' leading to the accession of the alternate heir and a desperate decision by the dead prince's widow to send her newborn son to safety far away. The suppression of the old king's will and a rewriting of birth dates to shore up the new monarch's claim to the throne.

It was a tale of treachery and the ruthless pursuit of power. But in his country's turbulent history, definitely possible.

How was it possible she'd found such a contentious document?

The likelihood was staggeringly remote. For centuries historians had plotted the family trees of the royal families in each of the neighbouring principalities.

Yet her earnestness, her straight-backed confidence caught his attention.

Obviously she'd found something. This woman was no one's fool, despite her up-tight demeanour. He remembered reading her CV when she had been recommended for the job of assessing and preserving the archives. Multiple qualifications. Glowing references. Her first degree in her teens and a formidable amount of experience since then.

It was tempting to believe this was a mistake, that she'd jumped to the wrong conclusion. Yet she didn't strike him as a woman prone to taking risks.

'You're not pleased?' she ventured, her brows puckering. 'I know it's a shock but—'

'But you thought I'd be thrilled to become king?' His words were clipped as he strove to suppress a surge of unfamiliar panic. He had to fight the rising nausea that clogged his throat.

He shook his head. 'I'm loyal to my cousin, Dr Connors. He will make the sort of king our country needs.'

Alaric succeeding in his place would be a nightmare made real.

Hell! The timing couldn't be worse. The country needed stability. If this was true...

'Who else have you told?' Alaric found himself on his feet, towering above her with his hands clamped on her chair arms. She shrank back as he leaned close.

In the flickering firelight she looked suddenly vulnerable and very young.

The pounding thud of his heartbeat slowed and he straightened, giving her space.

No need to intimidate the woman. Yet.

'I haven't told anyone.' Wide eyes stared at him from behind those ugly glasses and a twist of something like awareness coiled in his belly. 'I had to tell you first.'

The tension banding his chest eased and he breathed deep. 'Good. You did the right thing.'

Tentatively she smiled and he felt a tremor of guilt at having scared her. Even now one hand pressed to her breast as if her heart raced. He followed the rapid rise and fall of her chest. An unexpected trickle of fire threaded his belly as he recalled her feminine softness against him.

'When I get the test results back we'll know if the papers are what they seem to be.'

'Results?' He stilled. 'What tests are these?'

'There are several,' she said slowly, her expression wary. Alaric thrust his hand through his hair, fighting the impulse to demand she explain instantly.

Instead he took another deliberate step away from her and laid his forearm along the mantelpiece. Immediately the tension in her slim frame eased.

'Would you care to enlighten me?'

She blinked and blushed and for a moment Alaric was sidetracked by the softening of her lips as they formed an O of surprise. She looked charmingly female and innocently flustered in a way that threatened to distract him.

An instant later she was brisk and businesslike. 'I've sent pages for testing. We need to know if the parchment is as old as it appears. That it's not a modern forgery.'

She'd sent papers away? Who had them now? This got worse and worse.

'Plus the style of the text is unusual. I've sent copies of some pages to a colleague for verification.'

'Who gave you permission to do this?' His voice was calm, low, but with the razor edge honed on emergency decisions made under fire.

She jerked her head up, her body stiffening.

'I was told when I started that, so long as the usual precautions were taken, testing of documents found in the archives was allowed.'

'If you're right these aren't just any documents!' His hands fisted. Had she no notion of the powder keg she may have uncovered?

'That's why I was particularly careful.' She shot to her feet, hands clasped before her; chin lifted as she met his gaze. 'None of the pages I sent for testing were, by themselves, sensitive.' She paused then continued with slow emphasis. 'I realise this information must be kept confidential until it's confirmed. I followed the protocols set out when I took on the job.'

Alaric let out a slow breath. 'And if someone put those pages together?'

'No.' She shook her head then paused, frowning. 'It's not possible.' Yet she didn't look so certain.

Alaric determined to get his hands on the pages as soon as possible.

'It would have been better to keep this in house.' Even if it turned out this was a mistake, rumour could destabilise a delicate situation.

Fine eyebrows arched high on her pale forehead.

'Ruvingia doesn't have the capacity "in house" to run such tests.' She paused and he watched her drag in quick breaths, obviously battling strong emotion.

'I apologise if I've overstepped the mark.' Her tone said he was being unreasonable. 'I would have checked with you earlier but it's been hard getting an appointment.'

Touché. Meeting to discuss the royal archives hadn't been on his priorities.

'How long before you get the results?'

She launched into detail of how the document would be authenticated, her face growing animated. All the while he was busy reckoning the risks posed by this discovery. The need to verify her findings and keep the situation under wraps.

Yet he found himself watching her closely as she shed that shell of spiky reserve. There was a fire in her that had been lacking before. Or had it been hidden behind her starchy demeanour?

Despite the gravity of the situation, something in Alaric that was all male, functioning at the most primitive level, stirred.

Behind her dowdy appearance he sensed heat and passion in this woman.

He'd always been attracted by passion.

Alaric wrenched his mind back to the problem at hand.

'A short wait, then, before the results come through. In the meantime, who has access to this chronicle?'

'Only me. The assistant from your national museum is working on other material.'

'Good. We'll keep it that way.' Alaric would personally arrange for it to be kept under lock and key.

'I'm also keeping my eyes open for other papers that might confirm or disprove what I've found. There's still a lot to investigate.'

There could be more? Even if this document conveniently disappeared there might be others?

Damn. A simple solution had been tempting. An accident to destroy the evidence and remove the problem. Yet it would only make precautions around the remaining documents tighter and subsequent accidents more suspicious.

Self-knowledge warred with duty. The former told him the country would be better off in his cousin Raul's hands. The latter urged Alaric to face his responsibility no matter how unpalatable.

He speared a hand through his hair and paced, his belly churning. In thirty years he'd never shirked his duty, no matter how painful.

He'd warn Raul. They'd develop a contingency plan and make a discreet enquiry of the royal genealogist, a historian known for his expertise and discretion. Alaric needed to know if this far-fetched story was even possible.

Genuine or not, the papers were dynamite. If spare copies existed, and if Tamsin Connors was the innocent, earnest professional she appeared, he needed her onside.

If she was what she appeared.

Was it possible forged papers had been planted for her to find and disrupt Raul's coronation? Unlikely. Yet how convenient she'd found them after just a couple of weeks.

Too convenient?

He narrowed his gaze, taking in her heavy-framed glasses and appalling clothes. The way her gaze continually slipped away from his.

His gut tightened at the idea she was hiding something. A link to those stirring discontent? It was preposterous, but so was this situation.

He'd get to the bottom of it soon.

Meanwhile Tamsin Connors had his undivided attention.

'Of course, I understand,' Tamsin murmured into the phone.

She should be disappointed by the news she'd received. She *was* disappointed, but she was distracted by the man prowling the confines of the workroom. His long stride gave an impression of controlled impatience, at odds with his meticulous interest in every detail.

Intently she watched every move, miserably aware Prince Alaric didn't need a splendid uniform to show off his physique. In dark trousers, plain T-shirt and a jacket, he was compelling in the afternoon light.

Until last night she hadn't known she had a weakness for tall broad-shouldered men who looked like they could take on the world. For men whose eyes laughed one minute and clouded with grim emotion the next as if he saw things no man should.

She'd thought she preferred men driven by academic pursuits, preferably fresh faced and blond, like Patrick. Not sizzling with barely suppressed physical energy.

How wrong she'd been.

Her skin drew tight, every nerve end buzzing, as he paced.

'Thank you for calling. I appreciate it.' Carefully she put the phone down.

'A problem?' He approached, eyes watchful.

Tamsin dragged in a breath and placed her hands on the desk. She'd prayed her reaction last night had been an aberration. But seeing him in the flesh again scotched every hope that she'd imagined her response to his potent masculinity. His vitality, that sense of power and capability, were as fascinating as his stunning looks.

With his black hair, midnight-blue eyes, high-cut cheekbones and strong nose, he looked every inch the powerful aristocrat. Yet his mouth was that of a seducer: warm, provocative and sensual.

Tamsin blinked. Where had that come from?

'Dr Connors?'

'Sorry. I was…thinking.' Frantically she tried to focus. 'I've just heard the date test will be delayed.'

He frowned and she hurried on. 'I'd hoped for an early result on the age of the parchment but it will take longer than I'd hoped.'

The reasons she'd just been given were plausible. But the embarrassed way Patrick's assistant repeated herself made Tamsin suspicious.

Wasn't it enough Patrick had stolen the job that was by rights Tamsin's? He'd been the first man to show any interest in her, cruelly using her naïve crush to string her along. All those extra hours she'd put in helping him and he'd passed her work off as his own. He'd been promoted on the basis of it then dumped her unceremoniously. Pride had stopped her revealing his duplicity and her own lack of judgement. Instead she'd withdrawn even further into herself, nursing a bruised heart and vowing never to risk it again so readily.

Was he low enough to stymie this project, too?

Once it would never have occurred to her. Now she wondered if the whisper she'd heard was right and he saw her as a professional threat.

Would he really let ego get in the way of scientific research? The idea sickened her. How had she not seen his true character?

'They're returning the papers?' The prince's eyes sparked indigo fire and she watched, fascinated.

'Not yet. Hopefully it won't be a long delay.'

Tamsin watched his mouth compress. He was impatient. Despite what he'd said last night, he must be excited at the possibility of becoming king. Who wouldn't be?

'These are the rest of the newly found documents?' He gestured to the storage down one side of the long room.

'A lot of them. Some of the less fragile ones we've left until we can assess them properly.'

'Yet there may be more sensitive papers among them?'

'Possibly. But not many people would be able to read them. Even with my expertise, some of the texts are hard to decipher. It's time consuming and difficult.'

'That doesn't matter. We need secure storage for them all.' He strode restlessly down the room, assessing the set-up. Despite her intentions she followed every step, drinking in the sight of his powerful body. 'I want you to calculate exactly what you need and tell me today. They'll be locked with access only on my approval.'

Tamsin shook her head. 'It's not just a matter of space, it's about a properly regulated environment and—'

'I understand. Just let me know and it will be done.'

'It will be expensive.'

The prince waved a dismissive hand. He was notoriously wealthy. Money was no object now his self-interest was engaged.

Tamsin strove to stifle a pang of disappointment, recalling how her work had been virtually ignored earlier. She supposed his proprietorial attitude was justified. After all they were talking about proof of kingship. And if it meant proper care for the archives, all the better.

She stood. 'In the meantime, could I have the text to work on? I'll translate some more this evening.'

Late last night, after hearing her news, the prince had insisted on accompanying her here to see the original document. Then, without warning, and despite her protest, he'd taken it away. It worried her that he didn't fully appreciate how fragile it was.

'Certainly.' He glanced at his watch, obviously eager to be elsewhere. 'But not today—it's late.'

'But—'

He crossed the room to stand close, too close. She felt his heat, inhaled the spicy clean scent of his skin and wished she were still sitting.

'But nothing. I gather you've done little except work since you arrived. By your own admission this is taxing work.' He looked down at her with eyes that sparkled and a tremor rippled down her legs. Desperately she locked her knees, standing straighter.

'I'm not a slave driver and I don't want you making yourself ill working all hours.'

'But I want to!' What else did she have to do with her evenings?

He shook his head. 'Not tonight.' He turned and headed for the door, pausing on the threshold. 'If you could send me those storage requirements…'

'I'll see to it straight away.'

He inclined his head and left. Tamsin stood, swaying slightly and staring at the place where he'd been.

She'd hoped to spark his interest with her discovery. She hadn't thought to be sidelined in the process.

Sternly she told herself that wasn't what he'd done. She was allowing her experiences with one deceitful, good looking man to colour her judgement.

It was good of Prince Alaric to be concerned for her welfare. It was sensible that he took an interest in storing the documents properly.

So why did it feel like she was being outmanoeuvred?

Mid-evening Alaric headed for the gym on the far side of the castle compound. He needed to work off this pent up energy. His sleep patterns were shot anyway, but last night Tamsin Connors had obliterated any chance of rest.

The genealogist had warned today that proving or disproving a claim to the throne took time. Alaric wanted it sorted, and preferably disproved, *now*. It went against the grain to wait, dependent on forces beyond his control.

Plus, infuriatingly, his investigators had turned up little on the Englishwoman.

Surely no one had such a straightforward past? They'd reported on her academic achievements, her reputation for hard work and a little on her quiet childhood with elderly parents. But nothing about boyfriends. Any friends for that matter. Only an unconfirmed hint of some affair with a colleague.

In other circumstances he'd take her at face value: a quiet, dedicated professional. But he couldn't take chances. Not till he knew she was what she seemed.

She *seemed* too innocent to be believed.

He slowed as he passed the viewing level for the squash court. Lights were on and he paused to see which of the staff were playing.

There was only one. A woman, lithe and agile as she smashed the ball around the court in robust practice.

Alaric frowned, momentarily unable to place her. She lunged, twisting, to chase a low ball and for a moment her breasts strained against her oversized T-shirt. An instant later she pivoted on long legs with an agility he couldn't help but applaud.

His eyes lingered on the shapely length of those legs below baggy shorts. A sizzle of lazy heat ignited inside and he smiled appreciatively.

There was an age old remedy for insomnia, one he used regularly. A pretty woman and—

She spun round and a spike of heat drove through Alaric's torso, shearing off his breath.

He tensed instantaneously, hormones in overdrive.

It was Tamsin Connors. Yet not.

He should have guessed it was her, in those ill-fitting outfits. Yet she looked so different.

His mouth dried as he registered the amount of bare skin on view. Skin flushed pink and enticing from exertion. She really did have the most delicious legs. When that shirt twisted he realised her breasts were fuller than he'd guessed in her granny clothes. Her hair was soft around her face, escaping a glossy ponytail that swung like a sexy invitation to touch every time she moved. She breathed hard through her mouth, her lips not primmed any more, but surprisingly lush. Her eyes glittered—

Her eyes! No glasses.

Suspicion flared as he saw her face unmarred by ugly glasses. Maybe she wore contact lenses? But why hide the rest of the time behind disfiguring frames?

Had she tried to disguise herself? She'd done a remarkable job, concealing the desirable woman beneath a drab exterior and prickly professionalism.

Why? What had she to hide?

It was as if she deliberately tried to look like an absent-minded academic, absorbed in books rather than the world around her. She seemed too honest and serious to deceive. Yet instinct niggled, convincing him this was deliberate camouflage.

Alaric catapulted down the nearby stairs. On a bench beside the door to the court were an ugly cardigan and a case for glasses.

He flipped the latter open and held the glasses up to his face. Realisation corkscrewed through him and he swore under his breath. They gave only minuscule magnification.

Why did she wear them?

This time suspicion was a sharp, insistent jab. She was a stranger, in disguise. What a coincidence that she'd uncovered papers that could shatter the peace of the nation.

Tamsin Connors wasn't what she seemed. Was she part of a plot? An innocent dupe?

He'd just put the glasses down when she emerged.

Her thickly lashed eyes widened to bright dazzling amber, snaring his breath despite his anger. Amazing what those glasses had obscured. Her lips rounded in a soft pout of surprise and instantly fire exploded in his belly.

Slowly she approached.

Conflicting messages bombarded his brain. Caution. Distrust. Curiosity. Lust. *Definitely lust.*

His jaw hardened as he reined in that surge of hunger. This was no time to let his libido override his brain.

One thing was for certain. He wasn't going to let Tamsin Connors out of his sight till he got to the bottom of this. Already a plan formed in his head.

He smiled slowly in anticipation.

He and Dr Connors were about to become much more intimately acquainted.

CHAPTER THREE

TAMSIN'S steps faltered.

This man had invaded her thoughts, even haunted her dreams last night. Yet she'd forgotten how overwhelming he was in person.

So big. So vibrant. So powerfully *male*.

The air seemed to swirl and tickle her sensitised flesh as he subjected her to a short, all-encompassing survey. Heat blazed in her stomach and her skin tightened.

His eyes glittered and his mouth curved in welcome and her heart danced faster than it had on the squash court.

Would he look so welcoming if he knew she'd exhausted herself trying desperately to banish him from her thoughts? That she felt *excited* by his presence?

No. He paid her salary while she worked on loan here. He was her employer, an aristocrat living a glamorous, privileged life. A man with no interest in her or her work except that it made him eligible for the crown.

He'd be horrified by her reaction to him.

Even now her befuddled brain told her his smile wasn't a simple welcome. That it signified a deeper level of pleasure, a hint of danger. The sort of danger a sensible woman would ignore.

See? Her instincts were awry. She couldn't trust them.

Quickly she looked away, scared he'd read her thoughts. Patrick had read her longings like a book. She couldn't bear to reveal her weakness to this man, too.

The fact that she felt any weakness at all after the events of the last six months astounded her.

'Dr Connors.' His deep voice rippled like ruched velvet across her skin. She shivered, unable to suppress voluptuous pleasure at the sound.

Seeking distraction she reached for her cardigan and glasses, holding them close to her heaving chest.

'I hope you don't mind me using the court,' she murmured. 'Your steward said I could but I hadn't realised you might...'

'Of course I don't mind. It's good to see it in use. If I'd known you played I'd have invited you to a match.'

Startled, Tamsin looked up, straight into clear indigo depths that seemed warm and inviting.

He looked serious!

Her gaze strayed across muscled shoulders, down to the deep curve of a solid chest outlined against a black cotton T-shirt. She swallowed, her mouth drying at the latent power of him. His arms, tanned and strong, reminded her of the way he'd hoisted her over his shoulder as if she weighed nothing. Of how, despite her outrage, she'd revelled in his effortless he-man act.

He looked mouth-wateringly good in gym gear. As good as in uniform! It wasn't fair.

She stepped back, her eyes flicking away nervously.

'I don't think I'd be in your league.' Fervently she hoped he'd put her breathlessness down to her workout.

'I watched you play. You're quick and agile and know how to use your body.' His smile changed, became almost intimate, sending tendrils of heat winding around her internal organs. 'I'm sure we'd be very well matched.'

Tamsin's mind filled with an image of them matched in another way altogether. Tanned skin against pale. Hard masculine muscle against female softness.

Heat exploded, scalding her throat and face at the lurid, unfamiliar picture. Horrified, she ducked her head to fumble with her glasses case.

He couldn't know what she was thinking.

That didn't stop her embarrassment.

'It's kind of you to say so,' she mumbled. 'But we both know it would be an uneven match.'

She cast a furtive glance at his muscled arms and wished he'd cover himself up. It was hard not to stare.

'You underestimate yourself, Dr Connors.' His words sliced through her thoughts. 'Why is that? You struck me as a very confident woman when we discussed your work.'

Confident? She'd talked too much last night as they'd visited the archives. Nerves and guilt about the risks she'd taken with his books in the library had made her overcompensate. Anxiety had made her garrulous.

'That's different.' Reluctantly she lifted her chin and met his gaze. Even braced for the impact, the connection sent shock waves of pleasure racing through her. 'I've worked hard to develop my expertise. My work is what I'm good at. What I love.'

Tamsin had buried herself in work for years. At first because immersing herself in books had been an escape in her lonely childhood. Then from habit, especially as a student, when her age had set her apart from older colleagues. More recently it had been easier to be a workaholic than cultivate a personal life. She shivered. Her one foray into romance had been disastrous.

She waved a hand at the court. 'I lead a sedentary life. This is just a way to keep fit.' And a welcome outlet for troubled emotions.

He tilted his head, his gaze shrewd. 'Yet your focus was impressive. And your speed. You'd be a formidable opponent.'

The lazy approval was gone from his face, replaced by a seriousness that made her still.

Like last night Tamsin again had the suspicion he saw *her:* not just her academic reputation, but *whole*, talents and doubts, confidence and uncertainties. Saw the real person.

The notion thrilled yet made her feel oddly vulnerable.

She shoved an arm into her cardigan, pulled it round and slid her other arm in. Its familiarity steadied her, a reminder of her everyday world, devoid of handsome princes with dark chocolate voices.

She opened the case in her hands to take out her glasses. She felt naked meeting his scrutiny without them. But the sudden intensity of his stare arrested her. She closed the case with a snap.

'Hardly formidable, Your Highness. But thank you for the compliment.'

She made to turn away then stopped. This might be her only chance to talk to him. After today he'd probably be as elusive as before.

Steadfastly Tamsin ignored a sudden pang of disappointment. They had nothing in common. What did it matter if she never saw him again?

'Tomorrow, could I work on the text again? I'm eager to make more progress.'

'I'm sure you are.' Yet there was no answering enthusiasm in his face. If he was excited about the possibility of becoming monarch he hid it. His expression was flinty.

Had she said something wrong?

Finally he nodded. 'It will be brought to you tomorrow so you can pursue your…investigations.'

Tamsin sat absorbed, one bare foot tucked beneath her.

The more she delved into this manuscript, the more it fascinated. The choice of words, the phrasing, it was unique, even without the bombshell revelation that generations ago the wrong heir had become king. The intricate detail about life at court was incredible.

Take this word. She tilted her lamp to better view the idiosyncratic spelling. It should mean…

She paused, frowning as her thoughts strayed.

There was no sound, no movement on the periphery of her vision. Yet suddenly her focus was shot. The hairs on her arms prickled in atavistic awareness. Did she imagine a change in the atmosphere?

Tamsin focused again, trying to fathom the meaning of a convoluted sentence. Yet the more she tried to concentrate the more aware she became of…something else.

Finally in exasperation she looked up. And saw him.

The overhead lights were on against the fading afternoon. He stood under one, his black hair glossy in the spill of light. He was motionless, feet apart and hands in pockets in a masculine stance that reinforced the air of tough capability she'd noticed from the first.

Her heart throbbed an agitated tattoo. How long had he silently watched her? Why did he look so grim?

More than that, she wondered, as she sat back in her seat, what was he doing here?

'You've been working since seven-thirty this morning and you barely paused for lunch.' He dragged his hands from his pockets and approached. 'It's time you stopped.'

Tamsin frowned. 'You're keeping tabs on me?' She didn't feel indignant. She was too busy grappling with surprise.

He shrugged those superb shoulders and she stifled rising awareness. 'My staff have upped security given the importance of your find. I asked them to keep me informed.'

Informed of her meal breaks? Surely he had more on his mind than that? She opened her mouth to question him.

'You're translating?' He leaned over, one broad hand on the desk just inches from the manuscript.

Unaccountably heat washed her as she stared at his long fingers splayed close to hers. His masculine scent made her draw a deep, appreciative breath.

'Yes.' She sat straighter. 'It's a fascinating document, even apart from the succession issue.' She looked at the closely written text but all her attention was on the man who'd casually invaded her space.

'And now you've finished for the day.'

For a long moment Tamsin debated. It wasn't a question. She could contradict him and stay, working on the translation. Normally she worked much later. Yet her concentration had shattered. She found herself stretching, cramped muscles easing as she moved.

'Yes. I've finished.' She shoved her chair back and stood, busying herself packing up. By rights she should feel less overawed by him now she was on her feet. Instead, she inhaled his fresh scent as he leaned close and became aware of the way his body hemmed her in. It made her edgy.

'Good. You're free to come out.'

'Out?' Her brow knitted.

'How long since you left the castle?'

'I…' There had been her walk down to the river a few days ago. Or had it been a week? She'd been too busy to count days. 'I've been occupied lately.'

'As I thought.' He nodded. 'Come on. Pack that up.'

'I'm perfectly capable of getting fresh air myself.'

Eyes of dark sapphire held hers as he leaned across the desk. 'I'm sure you are. You're a most capable woman, Dr Connors.'

His mouth kicked up in a smile that lit his face and made her suck in her breath. The way he spoke her name, using her formal title as if it were an endearment, made her ridiculously flushed.

A warning bell clanged crazily in her head.

'Why are you here?' She braced her hands on the desk rather than lean towards that stunning smile. 'What do you want?'

She was no bedazzled fool, no matter how her pulse pattered out of control and illicit excitement shimmied along her backbone. Men like Prince Alaric didn't waste time on women like her. Women who weren't glamorous or sexy. She'd learned the hard way where she stood with the opposite sex and she wasn't making that mistake again.

'You don't pull your punches. I like your bluntness.'

Did he have any idea how gorgeous he looked, with laughter lines crinkling from his eyes and that conspiratorial grin turning rakishly handsome into devastatingly irresistible?

No wonder he had a reputation as a rogue. He'd only have to ask to get anything he wanted from a woman. The knowledge shored up her sagging defences.

She turned away to slip her notebook into a drawer.

'I do want something. I have a proposition for you.' She looked up, startled, and he raised a hand before she could interrupt. 'But not here. It's late. You need a break and I need to eat. I'll show you some of our Ruvingian hospitality and we can discuss it after we've eaten.'

Instinct warned her something was amiss. There was no reason for a prince to take an employee to dine. Yet the sparkle in his eyes invited her to forget her misgivings and take a chance.

Curiosity gnawed. What sort of proposition? Something to do with the archives?

'If you'd like someone to vouch for me…' he began.

Her lips twitched. 'Thank you, but no.'

Despite his easy charm there was a tension about his jaw that hinted at serious intent. Maybe what he had to say was important after all, not just a whim.

'Some fresh air would be welcome. And some food.' Suddenly she realised how hungry she was.

'Excellent.' He stepped back and the fragile sense of intimacy splintered. 'Wear warm clothes and comfortable shoes. I'll meet you by the garages in twenty minutes.'

'I'll see to this.' But as she reached for the text he pulled cotton gloves from his pocket and picked it up.

'I'll take care of that. You go and get ready.'

He didn't trust her to keep the chronicle safe. Last night he'd taken it away, saying he wanted it locked up. Disappointment was a plunging sensation inside her.

If he didn't trust her with that, how could he trust her to do her job? And why would he have a proposition?

Tamsin felt completely out of place in the luxurious, low-slung car as it purred out of the cobbled courtyard and over the bridge that connected the castle with the steep mountain spur. A last glimpse of the castle, a floodlit fantasy with its beautiful, soaring towers, reinforced her sense of unreality. She slid her fingers over the soft leather upholstery, eyes wide as she took in the state of the art controls. She'd never been in a car like this.

Or spent time alone with a man like Prince Alaric.

In the confines of the vehicle he was impossible to ignore. So big and vital. Electricity charged the air so it buzzed and snapped. It was hard to breathe.

She told herself lack of food made her light-headed. She should have eaten lunch instead of skimping on an apple.

He nosed the car down a series of swooping bends and she risked a sideways look. A smile played around his mouth as if an icy road after dusk was just what he loved. His powerful hands moved easily on the wheel, with a fluid sureness that hinted he enjoyed tactile pleasures.

Tamsin shivered as an unfamiliar yearning hit her.

'You're cold?' He didn't take his eyes off the road. How had he sensed the trawling chill that raked her spine?

'No, I'm warm as toast.'

'So it's the road that bothers you.' Before she could answer he eased his foot onto the brake.

It was on the tip of her tongue to protest. He hadn't been speeding. She'd enjoyed the thrill of the descent, instinctively sensing she was safe with such a capable driver. Disappointment rose as they took the next bend at a decorous pace but she didn't contradict him. She didn't want to try explaining the curious feelings that bombarded her when she was with him.

'What's this proposition you have for me?'

He shook his head, not looking away from the road as it curved one final time then disappeared like a dark ribbon into the forest at the foot of the mountain. 'Not yet. Not till we've eaten.'

Tamsin tamped down her impatience, realising her companion had no intention of being swayed. For all his light-hearted charm she sensed he could be as immoveable as the rock on which his castle perched.

'Tell me why you took this position. Being cooped up here in the dead of winter hasn't got much to recommend it.'

Was he kidding? Tamsin slanted another glance his way and saw nothing but curiosity in his expression.

'The place is beautiful. Its heritage listed for outstanding scenic and cultural significance.'

'But you've barely been out of the castle.'

Tamsin stiffened. Had his staff been reporting her movements? Why? The unsettling discovery didn't sit well with the sense of freedom she'd enjoyed.

'I'd planned to explore. But once I got engrossed in my work and found Tomas's chronicle, I never found time.'

'You came to Ruvingia for the views?' Disbelief edged his tone.

'Hardly.' Though the picturesque setting was a bonus. 'It was the work that fascinated me.'

'You don't mind spending an alpine winter so far from family and friends?'

Tamsin looked away, to the dark forest crowding close. She was grateful for the heating which dispelled any chill. 'My parents were the first to urge me to apply. They know how important my work is to me.'

They didn't care about her not being home for the festive season. As far as her father, a single-minded academic, was concerned the holidays were simply a nuisance that closed the university libraries. Her mother, wrapped up in her art, found it easier catering for two than three. Theirs was a distant kind of caring. They were dedicated to their work and Tamsin, an unexpected child after years of marriage, had fitted between the demands of their real interests. She'd grown self-sufficient early, a dreamer losing herself in a world of books.

'What about your friends? Surely you'd rather be with them at this time of year?' He probed the sore point, making her want to shrink inside herself.

Tamsin had friends, but none were particularly close.

Except Patrick. She'd expected to see a lot of him over the holidays. Had expected their relationship to blossom into something wonderful.

Before she'd discovered what a gullible idiot she'd been.

She turned to find Prince Alaric watching her closely. In the dim interior light she sensed an intensity to his stare that surprised her. Why did this interest him so?

'You don't understand how exciting this job is.' With an effort she pinned on a bright smile. 'A previously unknown hoard of documents. The opportunity to be of real value, preserving what might otherwise be lost. Not to mention the excitement of discovery. The chance to…' She hesitated, unwilling to reveal how important this job was at a more personal level.

This had been an escape route she'd gratefully seized. She couldn't bear Patrick gloating over his success and sneering at her naivety. Plus there'd been her colleagues' pitying looks.

It was also an opportunity to shore up her battered self-esteem. To prove that despite her appalling lapse of judgement with Patrick, she was good at what she did. Even, she admitted now, to show those who'd doubted her abilities they'd made a mistake promoting Patrick instead of her. His work was inferior but he had the charm to make the most of every opportunity. They'd soon realise their mistake but Tamsin wouldn't be human if she didn't want to banish her growing self-doubts with a coup of her own.

'The chance to…?'

Tamsin dragged herself back to the conversation. What had she been saying? 'The chance to be part of this exciting discovery. It's a once in a lifetime opportunity.'

'But you can't have known that when you applied for the job.' His riposte was lightning fast. He speared her with a penetrating look before turning back to the road.

'No, but I…'

She couldn't tell him how desperately she'd needed to escape. Escape Patrick lording his new position over her; Patrick with his old girlfriend on his arm again. Her forlorn heart had shredded whenever she'd seen them.

'I wanted a change. This sounded too good to miss.' She sounded stilted, falsely bright, but she wasn't about to bare her soul.

'Too good to be true, in fact.' His voice deepened on a curiously rough note. In the streetlights of the town they'd entered he looked stern.

Had he grown bored? He was probably used to more scintillating conversation. Tamsin was more than happy to change the subject.

'Where are we going?' They were in the old town, where roads narrowed and cobblestones glistened. Lights were strung between lampposts, giving the streets a festive air as pedestrians strolled, looking at decorated shop windows.

Tamsin wished she could be one of them. Away from prying questions. Away from memories that taunted her.

'The winter market is on,' he said. 'We'll eat and you can see some of the sights.'

Tamsin felt a flicker of excitement. The town looked quaintly romantic with half-timbered houses, brightly painted shutters and steep, snow-capped roofs.

But with a prince by her side relaxation was impossible. Instead she fretted over his mysterious proposition and the growing sense of something wrong. Why this interest in her?

A couple strolled hand in hand across the street, catching her eye. They were barely aware of anyone else, completely absorbed in each other. She felt a small pang of envy. Once she'd hoped she and Patrick…

Tamsin had never been close to anyone like that. Never experienced all-encompassing love, even from her parents. Never even fitted in, finishing school before her age peers and being so much younger than her university colleagues.

She turned away, setting her mouth firmly. She refused to pine for what she'd never had. One perilous venture into romance had proved what she'd always suspected. Love wasn't for her. She just didn't inspire that sort of affection.

But she had her work. That was compensation enough.

Alaric viewed the woman beside him with frustration. Two hours in her company and she was still an enigma.

On one level she was easy to read. Her peal of laughter at the antics of children on the outdoor ice-skating rink. Her enthusiasm for markets filled with local handcrafts and produce. She was pleased by simple delights: watching a woodcarver create a nutcracker dragon, or a lace-maker at work, asking questions all the time.

Most women he knew would complain of the rustic entertainment!

It was tempting to believe her innocent of deception.

But she'd prevaricated in the car and he'd sensed there was more to her reasons for coming here. Her tension when he pushed for answers, and the way she avoided his gaze made him suspicious.

She was back in disguise, hiding behind thick-rimmed glasses and a scrunched up bun, with an anorak the wrong colour for her complexion and a pair of shapeless trousers.

Was she trying to banish any memory of her in shorts?

His mouth twisted grimly. That particular image was emblazoned on his brain.

With rapt attention she watched a stallholder cook pancakes and fill them with dark cherries, walnuts and chocolate. It was pure pleasure watching her. Her face was blissful as she bit into the concoction, oblivious to the sauce glistening on her bottom lip or Alaric's testosterone-induced reaction as it dripped to her chin.

She swiped her lips with a pink tongue. To his horror his groin tightened and throbbed as if she'd stripped her ugly clothes away and offered him her soft body.

Right here. Right now…

What was going on? She was nothing like his usual women. He wasn't even sure he could trust her.

Yet her combination of quick mind, buttoned up formality, prickly challenge and hidden curves was absurdly, potently provocative.

She was like a special treat waiting to be unwrapped. The perfect diversion for a man jaded by too many easy conquests. Too many women seeking to trap him with practised seduction and false protestations of love.

Someone bustled past, bumping her close and branding her body against his. His mouth dried. He had to force himself to let go after he'd steadied her.

'Come,' he said abruptly. 'Let's find somewhere quiet.'

Tamsin looked up at his brusque tone, pleasure waning as she read his stony expression. Clearly he'd had enough.

She couldn't blame him. He'd gone out of his way to show her sights that must, for him, be unremarkable. Plus all evening he'd been approached by citizens eager to talk. He'd had no respite.

To her dismay her hackles had risen at the number of women who'd approached him, simpering and laughing when he turned his blue eyes in their direction. What did that say about her? Hastily she shoved away her petty annoyance at them.

She'd watched fascinated as he handled requests with good humour and practicality. He made his royal obligations look simple. She noticed he didn't have any obvious minders with him but mixed easily with the crowd. Perhaps his security staff blended in.

'Of course,' she murmured. 'Somewhere quiet would be—'

A crack of sound reverberated, then a shout. Her breath caught as a young boy raced in front of her, skidding on the cobbles and catapulting towards a vat of simmering spiced wine. She cried out, instinctively reaching for him.

A large figure plunged forward as the cauldron teetered. It overturned just as Alaric hauled the youngster away. There was a crash, a sizzle of hot liquid and a cry of distress, then a cloud of steam as the boy was thrust into her hands.

In the uproar that followed Tamsin lost sight of the prince as the crowd surged forward. Then, out of the confusion he appeared, pocketing his wallet and nodding to the smiling stallholder. He accepted thanks from the boy's parents but didn't linger. Moments later he propelled Tamsin across the square and into an old hotel.

Only when they were ushered into a private dining room did Tamsin see his face clearly. It was white, the skin stretched taut across sculpted bones, his lips bloodless.

'Are you all right?'

It was clear he wasn't. Rapidly she scanned him, looking for injury. That's when she noticed the large splash staining his hand and her stomach turned over.

Tamsin propelled him to the bench seat lining one wall. He subsided and she slid in beside him, moistening a linen napkin from a water carafe and pressing it to his hand.

He sat silent and unmoving, staring ahead.

Tamsin washed the wine away, revealing a burn to the back of his hand. She pressed the wet cloth to it again.

'Is it just your hand? Where else does it hurt?'

Slowly he turned his head, looking blankly at her. His eyes were almost black, pupils dilated.

'Your Highness? Are you burned elsewhere?' She cupped his hand, reassured by the warmth of his skin against hers, though the chill distance in his eyes worried her. Frantically she patted his trousers with her other hand, testing for more sticky wine.

Finally he looked down.

Her hand stilled, splayed across the solid muscle of his thigh. Suddenly her eagerness to help seemed foolish.

'I'm fine. No other burns.' He threw the wet cloth onto the table, drawing a deep breath as colour seeped along his cheek-bones. His free hand covered hers, sandwiching it against living muscle that shifted beneath her palm.

Fire licked Tamsin's skin. Something curled tight inside her at the intimacy of that touch.

Ink blue eyes surveyed her steadily and long fingers threaded through hers, holding her hand prisoner. Tingles of awareness shimmied up her arm to spread through her body.

'In the circumstances you can forget the title.' His voice was as smooth and seductive as the cherry chocolate sauce she still tasted on her lips. 'Call me Alaric.'

His mouth lifted in a tiny smile that made Tamsin's insides liquefy. A smile that hinted at dangerous intimacies, to match that voice of midnight pleasures.

Abruptly she leaned back, realising she'd swayed unthinkingly towards him.

'You're sure you're not hurt?' Her voice was scratchy, as if it were she who'd lunged in to save the boy, not him. The blankness had gone from his face as if it had never been, yet she couldn't help wondering what secrets lurked behind his apparently easy smile.

'Positive. As for this...' he flexed his burned hand '...it's fine. Though thank you for your concern.' He leaned forward, eyes dancing. Had she imagined those moments of rigid shock? It had seemed so profound. So real.

'Now we're alone, we can talk about my proposition.' He was so close his breath feathered her hair and cheek. Tamsin had to fight not to shiver in response.

'Yes, Your…yes, Alaric.' She strove for composure, despite the wayward excitement that welled, being so close to him. 'What did you have in mind?'

His fingers flexed around hers. His strength surrounded her. It was strangely comforting despite the way her nerves jangled at the look in his eyes.

His smile broadened and her breath snared.

'I want you to be my companion.'

CHAPTER FOUR

'Your...companion?' Tamsin snapped her mouth shut before she could say any more.

He *couldn't* mean what she thought.

Companion could have all sorts of interpretations. It was shaming proof of the way he turned her brain to mush that she'd immediately thought he meant *lover*.

Her heartbeat ratcheted up a notch and her breathing shallowed as, unbidden, another graphic picture filled her brain. The two of them, stretched naked on the carpet before the fire in his library. Limbs entwined. Lips locked. His hard, capable hands shaping her body.

Was that answering heat in his eyes? He watched her so closely. Could he guess her thoughts?

Tamsin forced her breathing to slow and sat straighter. She reminded herself she was known for her analytical mind. Not flights of fantasy.

He kept her hand anchored against him. Foolishly she couldn't bring herself to pull it away.

'That's right.' He nodded.

Companion to Prince Alaric of Ruvingia. Women would kill for time with Europe's most notorious bachelor. For the chance to persuade him into marriage or just to experience his vaunted expertise as a lover.

Desperately Tamsin told herself she wasn't one of them.

'You've mistaken me for someone else.' She lifted her chin, bracing for the moment he told her this was a joke.

Instead he shook his head.

'No mistake, Dr Connors.' He paused, his lips pursing ruminatively. To her horror, Tamsin couldn't take her eyes off his mouth. 'Perhaps I'd better call you Tamsin.'

A delicious little shudder tickled every nerve ending as he said her name like that.

As if it pleased him.

As if he looked forward to saying it again.

Reality crashed down in a moment of blinding insight. *He was playing with her.* A man like him would never view a woman like her in that light.

'Feel free.' She forced her voice not to wobble. 'What is it you're proposing?'

One straight brow lifted, giving him a faintly superior air. 'Exactly what it sounds. I need a companion and you'd be perfect. There'd be benefits for you too.'

Tamsin resisted the impulse to shake her head to clear her hearing. She'd watched him speak. She knew what he'd said. The excited patter of her pulse was testament to that.

No man had described her as *perfect* before.

'My invitation this evening wasn't totally altruistic,' he continued.

Did he realise he'd begun absent-mindedly stroking the back of her hand with his thumb as he clamped it to his leg? 'I wanted to see if we're compatible.'

'Compatible?'

His lips stretched in a brilliant smile that made something flip over inside. Only the hooded intelligence in his bright stare hinted this wasn't as simple as it seemed.

Sternly Tamsin told herself to be sensible. Logical. All the things she didn't feel when he touched her, smiled at her like that.

'I need a companion who won't bore me in the first half-hour.'

'I take it I passed muster?' Anger ignited at the notion of being assessed. Had it occurred to him she might have better things to do with her time?

She was sure she'd think of them in a minute.

She tugged her hand but he didn't release it.

His expression sobered. 'I needed to be sure you'd handle it, too. It's not necessarily fun keeping me company while I play prince-in-residence for all comers.'

Tamsin stared, curious at the bitterness in his voice as he spoke of his princely role. Was it real or feigned?

'I wasn't bothered.' She'd felt privileged to be with him and to see the able way he'd dealt with requests from the light-hearted to the serious. He had an easy manner with people. She envied that. 'But I still don't understand.' She took a deep breath and willed herself to concentrate. 'Why do you need a companion? And why me?'

'Ah, I knew you'd go to the crux of things.'

Alaric watched her troubled face and realised he'd have to do better. He'd only aroused her suspicions.

He supposed it was the shock of rescuing the boy that had done it. The initial explosion of sound: probably a firecracker but for an instant so like the report of a firearm. The need for urgent action combined with the feel of those small, bony shoulders beneath his hands, the distress on the kid's face. The huge, fearful dark eyes that for a moment had looked so hauntingly familiar. Together they'd triggered memories Alaric usually submerged beneath the everyday demands on his time.

It had only taken seconds, but that was enough to tip the balance and slide him into a nightmare world of guilt and pain. In an instant he'd been back in another time, another place. To another life he'd been unable to save.

Only the touch of Tamsin's hands, the concern in her voice and her insistence had dragged him out of a state he'd prefer not to think about. It was a condition he usually managed alone, never sharing with others.

That was the way it would stay.

'Commitments mean I'm staying in Ruvingia for a while.'

She nodded, wariness in every line of her face.

'And…' He paused, wondering how best to phrase this. How to appeal to this woman he couldn't read? 'While I'm here I need a companion.'

Amber eyes regarded him unblinkingly through the lenses of her glasses.

'Why? You can't be lonely.'

Couldn't he?

No matter how frenetically he'd pursued pleasure through Europe's glittering capitals, no matter how many lovers warmed his bed, Alaric remained profoundly alone. And when he was alone the memories came. Hence his constant need for action, for diversion.

She didn't need to know any of that.

'Not lonely, precisely.' He favoured her with a smile that had won him countless women.

She appeared unmoved, staring back with a slight frown as if she couldn't quite place him in a catalogue. Irritation surfaced. Why couldn't she be like the rest and fall in with his wishes? Why did she have to question everything?

Yet there was something about her seriousness, about the fact that she held herself aloof, that appealed.

'It would make my life easier if I were seen out and about with the same woman. A woman who didn't expect that to lead to a more permanent arrangement.'

As he said it, Alaric realised how weary he'd become of socialites and trophy mistresses. It would be a relief to be with someone who didn't fit the conventional mould of glossy beauty and vacuous conversation.

She tilted her head to one side, her mouth flattening primly. 'You want a decoy? Because you're tired of being chased by women out to snare you?'

'You could say that.' He shrugged and watched her gaze flicker away. 'There's something about a royal title that attracts women eager to marry.'

'I'd have thought you could cope with that.' Her words were tart. 'You've got a reputation for enjoying yourself in short term relationships. Surely you don't need to hide behind any woman.'

He read the stiffness in her body and realised he'd have to offer more. There was no sympathy there. If anything she looked disapproving.

'These are delicate times, Tamsin.' He lingered on her name, liking the sound of it. 'Power blocs are jockeying for position and they include some aristocratic families who'd love to cement their status by linking to royalty.'

'Marriage to you, you mean?'

He nodded. 'I've had aristocratic ladies paraded before me for months and it's getting harder to avoid them.'

'You're an adult. You just have to say you're not interested!' She tried to withdraw her hand but he refused to relinquish it. This wasn't going as he'd anticipated.

'It's not so simple. Even a rumour that one contender is favoured over another could change the perceived balance of power. My cousin Raul is under the same pressure.'

Alaric leaned forward, using his most cajoling tone. 'All I'm asking is some help to keep them at a distance. Is that unreasonable?'

Her lips thinned and she surveyed him coolly.

Impatience spiked. He was tempted to cut through her questions and demand acquiescence the easy way.

He'd drag her glasses away, cup her head in his hand and kiss her till her mouth grew soft and accommodating and she surrendered to his wishes. Till she blushed a delicate pink all over as she had on the squash court, this time with pleasure and anticipation.

Till she capitulated and said she'd do whatever he wanted.

Anything he wanted.

Heat poured through him as he remembered her parted lips, ripe with cherries. The swipe of her tongue licking up sauce in a move so innocently sexy it had tugged him towards arousal. The feel of her breasts against him as he carried her down the library ladder.

Alaric's pulse quickened, his hold on her hand tightening.

'I can see it might be useful to have someone to keep other women away.' Her tone told him her sympathy was limited. 'But what's that got to do with me?'

'You're already here living at the castle. You're not impressed by my position.' Despite the importance of persuading her, Alaric's lips twitched as he saw her flush. Few women could have made it clearer his title and money meant nothing. She had no notion how refreshing that was. To be viewed as just a man. 'You won't get ideas about companionship turning to something more.'

He raised her hand to his lips and kissed it, inhaling the summery fragrance of her satin skin, enjoying the little shiver of awareness she couldn't hide. Tamsin was different from other women. He couldn't remember any of them intriguing him so. Protecting his country had never coincided so well with personal inclination.

They said you should keep your friends close and your enemies closer. Alaric wasn't sure yet if she was an enemy or an innocent, but he'd enjoy keeping Tamsin Connors close. Very close.

Tamsin's heart faltered and seemed to stop as his lips caressed her hand in a courtly gesture. The trouble was, to her overwrought senses it felt provocative, not courtly, evoking reactions out of proportion with the circumstances.

There was no mistaking the amusement in his eyes. He was laughing at her. Did he take her for a fool?

She yanked her hand away, anger and hurt bubbling in a bitter brew that stung the back of her throat.

'No one would believe it.'

'Why not? People will believe their eyes.'

She shook her head, wishing he'd stop this game.

'Tamsin?' He frowned and she realised she was blinking eyes that felt hot and scratchy. Hurriedly she looked away at the old mural of convivial wine makers on the far wall.

'I'm not the sort of woman to be companion to a prince.' Even if it was make-believe.

'I know my record with women is abysmal but surely you could make an exception in the circumstances.'

'Oh!' She shot to her feet. 'Just stop it!' Tamsin paced the room then whirled to face him. 'No one would ever believe you'd really taken up with someone like…' The words choked as her throat constricted. 'Like me.'

He rose, eyes fixed on hers. 'Nonsense.'

Tamsin felt like stamping her foot. Or shouting.

Or curling up in a ball and crying her eyes out.

All the weak, emotional things she'd wanted to do when Patrick had revealed he'd only spent time with *a woman like her* because she was useful to his ambitions. All the things she hadn't let herself do because she'd been busy pretending it didn't matter.

'Look at me.' She gestured comprehensively to her practical, unglamorous clothes. 'I'm not…' But she couldn't go on. She knew she wasn't attractive, that she didn't inspire thoughts of romance or even plain old lust. But she refused to say it out loud. She had some pride.

'I see a woman who's intelligent and passionate and intriguing.' His words snapped her head up in disbelief.

When had he moved so close?

He loomed over her, making the room shrink so it seemed there was only her and him in a tiny, charged space.

Tamsin's throat worked as anger roiled. 'I refuse to be the butt of your joke.' She swung away but he caught her elbow, turning her implacably to face him.

'It's no joke, Tamsin. I was never more serious.'

She angled her chin higher. 'I don't think my clothes would pass muster for consorting with royalty, do you?' Easier to focus on that than the shortcomings of the woman who wore them.

'I don't give a damn about your clothes,' he growled, a frown settling on his brow. 'If they bother you replace them. Or let me do it if you don't have the cash.'

'Oh, don't be absurd!' As if it was just the clothes. Tamsin knew how men viewed her. No one would believe she was a sexpot who'd snared the interest of a playboy prince!

'Absurd?' The single word slid, lethally quiet into the vibrating silence, raising the hairs on her nape.

His eyes sparked fire. Suddenly the danger she'd once sensed in him was there, staring down at her.

A frisson of panic crept through her.

She backed a step. He followed.

'You don't believe me?'

Silently she shook her head. Of course she didn't believe him. She had no illusions. She—

In one stride he closed the gap between them. His hands cupped her face, fingers sliding into her hair, dislodging pins. The sensation of him tunnelling through her hair, massaging her scalp was surprisingly sensual.

Tamsin stared up into eyes darkening to midnight-blue, so close she could barely focus. She told herself to move away but found her will sapped by the look in his eyes. The floor seemed to drop away beneath her feet as she read his expression, his fierce intent.

That look bewildered her. She'd never seen it before.

'I—'

Her words stopped as his lips crushed hers. She gasped, inhaling his scent and the spicy taste of his skin. Her thoughts unravelled.

Taking advantage of her open mouth Alaric devoured her. He was determined, skilful, dominant. He overwhelmed every sense, blotted out the world. Stole her away to a place of dark ecstasy unlike any she'd known.

He held her so firmly she couldn't move. His body was hard, awakening unfamiliar sensations that rippled and spread, a trickle turning into a torrent of excitement.

Dimly Tamsin realised she didn't want to move. That in fact her hands had crept up around his neck, linked there to stop herself falling. Neither did she mind the sense of him surrounding her, legs planted wide to anchor them both. Her eyes closed as her thoughts scrambled.

Bliss beckoned.

This was nothing like Patrick's lukewarm attentions. Or the hesitant clumsiness she'd felt in his embrace.

For the first time Tamsin felt passion burst into scorching life. All she could do was acquiesce. And enjoy.

His kiss was fervent, almost angry, yet Tamsin had never known such delight. He ravished her mouth so fiercely she trembled with the force of it, bowed backwards as he surged forward, seemingly unable to slake his need.

And she welcomed him.

Despite his sudden aggressive ardour she wasn't afraid. Instead it made her feel…powerful.

Vaguely she wondered at that, but her mind refused to compute the implications. She simply knew that with Alaric she was safe. Even if it was like stepping off a skyscraper into nothingness. His strong arms hauled her close and she gave herself to delight.

She kissed him back, revelling in the warm sensuality of their mouths melding. He licked her tongue and she moaned, her knees quaking at the impact of this sensual onslaught.

The kiss altered. He didn't bend her back quite so ferociously, though he still strained against her. His hungry ardour eased into something more gentle but no less satisfying.

She breathed deep as he planted kisses along her jaw. Sensation bloomed with each caress. Her skin tingled and her breasts grew heavy. She thrust herself against him, needing his hardness just there. Her breath came in desperate gasps as she struggled to fill air-starved lungs. She clung tight, wanting more.

He moved to kiss her on the mouth again and bumped her glasses askew.

Instantly he froze. As if that simple action reminded him who he was kissing. Not a svelte sophisticate but plain Tamsin Connors.

He stilled, lips at the sensitive corner of her mouth. Tamsin held her breath, desperate for him to kiss her again. Craving more of his magic.

His steely embrace loosened and firm hands clasped her shoulders, steadying her as if he knew her legs felt like stretched elastic. He pulled back and she swayed, bereft of his heat and strength.

A protest hovered on her swollen lips but she swallowed it. She would not beg for more. Not now she saw the dawning horror on his face. The unmistakeable regret in the way his gaze slid to her mouth then away.

'Are you OK?' His voice was gruff, his expression stern. He was embarrassed, she realised.

Pity had provoked the kiss, but the reminder of who it was he embraced had stopped him in his tracks.

The lovely, lush taste of him turned to ashes on her tongue. The thrill that had hummed through her with every caress died.

There was no magic. It had been a kindness gone wrong. *An act of charity from a man who felt sorry for her.*

Anger and regret chased each other in a sickening tumble of emotions. At least, she told herself, he hadn't deliberately set out to dupe her, like Patrick.

She'd duped *herself* into believing that kiss was real.

Now she had to pick up the pieces. Pretend it didn't matter that he'd unthinkingly awoken heart-pounding desire in a woman who'd never known its like before.

Tamsin wanted to howl her despair.

But she had the torn remnants of her dignity. She might only be suitable as a decoy, not wanted for herself, but he needn't know he'd shredded her self-respect.

Deliberately she lifted a hand to set her glasses straight on her face. It was a gesture of habit, but never had it held such significance.

'I'm fine, thank you, Alaric. How are you?'

Alaric stared at the cool-eyed woman before him and struggled with his vocal cords. They'd shut down, just like his brain when he'd hauled her into his arms and slammed his mouth against hers.

Even now he was barely in control of himself! One moment of madness had turned into something more. Something that threatened the boundaries he used to keep from feeling, from engaging fully in the world around him.

He'd kissed countless women but not one had made him *feel*. Not like this.

Who the hell was she? What had she done to him? Passion was a pleasure, a release, an escape. Never had it overwhelmed him like that.

'You're sure?' He sounded strangled, like an untried teen, hot and bothered by his first taste of desire.

'Of course.' Her brows rose in splendid indifference. As if being accosted by lust-ridden strangers was an inconsequential distraction.

Alaric scrubbed a hand over his face, annoyed to note the slight tremor in his fingers.

Tamsin Connors might dress like someone's ancient maiden aunt but she kissed with all the generous ardour any man could want. The feel of her lush body melting against his, her mouth hot and welcoming, had driven away the last shred of his sanity. Their passion had been volcanic.

Hard now to believe her apparent hurt and self-doubt had appalled and angered him. It had provoked him into doing what he'd wanted for so long now: kiss the woman silent. When he'd dislodged her glasses he'd come to his senses and been horrified at the idea he'd taken advantage of her. Possibly scared her.

Had her earlier pain been real? Or had she played on his sympathies?

It infuriated him that he was no closer to understanding her. She was a bundle of contradictions. Fiery yet reserved. Confident in professional matters yet still vulnerable. Thrilled by a rustic fair but unimpressed by his title. A siren who shattered his control like no other.

He wanted to rip away the façade she presented the world and uncover the real Tamsin Connors.

He wanted to run from what she made him feel.

But mostly he wanted her back in his arms.

He drew a deep breath. One thing he knew for certain. *She was the most dangerous woman he knew.*

'I apologise,' he said stiffly. 'I shouldn't have done that.'

'No, you shouldn't.' She glared at him and it was all he could do not to reach for her again. With her eyes snapping gold fire, her hair in tumbled waves around her shoulders and her lips red-dened and full she was too alluring. Even the glasses couldn't hide that now.

How had he ever thought her ordinary?

'As I said, Tamsin,' he lingered appreciatively over her name, 'clothes are immaterial.' He watched colour flush her cheeks and felt savage pleasure that she wasn't as unmoved as she pretended. 'I look for more than fashion in a woman.'

'I'm not *anyone's* woman.' Her chin angled up.

'Just as well,' he murmured, as something primitively posses-sive surfaced. 'We wouldn't want the complication of a jealous boyfriend, would we?'

'No fear of that.'

She looked away. Her expression didn't change but suddenly he regretted baiting her to salve his pride. Whatever had happened, whoever she really was, Tamsin had been caught like him in the conflagration erupting between them. At least he hoped so. The alternative was unthinkable.

'You're surely not still serious about this?'

'Never more so.' He watched her turn. She drew a slow breath as if gathering herself.

'You said if I spent time with you there'd be a benefit in it for me.' Her voice was crisp, her demeanour completely business-like. 'What did you mean?'

Disappointment reared at her about-face; her obvious self-interest. Alaric told himself it was easier to deal with her now than when she was warm and willing in his arms. A pity he didn't believe it.

'I've been thinking about the job we've contracted you to do. It would be easier if you had more staff.'

The light in her eyes told him he'd finally snared her interest. He squashed a spark of annoyance that he came second in her priorities to a pile of mouldering books.

'Not easier, but there's a chance of further damage in the time it takes us to assess what we've got.' She chewed her lower lip. Heat scorched Alaric's lower body as he focused on its softened contours. In repose Tamsin's mouth was a perfect Cupid's bow of invitation.

'The offer only applies if I become your *companion*?' The twist of her lips and her chilly look told him how little she liked the prospect. 'That sounds like blackmail.'

Alaric shrugged. His gaze drifted to her mouth and he remembered her moan of delight as they'd kissed. She only feigned disinterest.

'If you agree it will mean some time away from your work. Putting extra resources into the archives will compensate. Two qualified full time staff.' He watched excitement light her face.

'And you may want to come with me when I open a new wing of the national museum. There's a collection behind the

scenes that may interest you. Illuminated gospels that I believe
are noteworthy.' Those treasures had never been outside the
country. Neither had foreign experts viewed them.

Her eyes widened eagerly. In other women it was the sort of
look reserved for a gift of emeralds or rubies.

Tamsin Connors was unique. In far too many ways.

'This…arrangement would only interrupt my work occa-
sionally?'

Alaric gritted his teeth. Women vied for his attention. He'd
never needed to bribe one to be with him!

'That's right.'

Still she hesitated. She clasped her hands before her in a gesture he'd come to realise signalled vulnerability.

'We're not talking about anything more than spending time
together? Being seen in public?'

He nodded curtly.

'Then…' She paused and licked her lip as if her mouth had
dried. Alaric's groin tightened as he remembered her lush sweetness. 'Then I accept. On one condition.'

'Yes?' He hauled his gaze from her mouth.

The glacial expression he found in her eyes would have frozen
a lesser man.

'No more kisses. Nothing…intimate.'

Alaric bowed stiffly, all dignity and insulted pride.

'You have my word that I won't take advantage. Nothing
intimate except at your express request.'

She pretended to abhor his touch?

She'd soon be on her knees begging for his kisses.

CHAPTER FIVE

'I'M SORRY, ma'am. You can't go this way.'

Tamsin looked at the burly man blocking the path and drew her jacket close. His wide stance and implacable stare made the crisp morning feel chillier. Or was it that he automatically spoke in heavily accented English? As if he knew who she was and had been waiting for her?

'Why not?' This was the path to the village and she needed a walk to clear her head. After days working long hours she was no closer to finding the peace she'd always taken for granted in her job.

That peace had been missing since *he'd* taken her out four days ago. Since he'd kissed her till her head swam and her senses reeled and she'd forgotten she was plain Tamsin Connors. Since he'd proposed a fake relationship then promptly disappeared, leaving her wondering if she'd conjured the idea as a wish-fulfilling fantasy.

Each day she'd waited, nerves on edge, for him to summon her. Only to learn today he was away in the capital.

It rankled that he'd left without telling her. As if he had to report his movements! Yet after what he'd said she'd expected to see more of him.

Not that she was disappointed.

It was just that she wanted to work on the chronicle. She couldn't access it in his absence. *That's* what frustrated her.

'A landslip has taken part of the path.'

The stranger didn't move his eyes off her, neither did he smile. Tamsin's gaze strayed to his walkie-talkie. He didn't look like a groundsman, more like heavy duty security.

'How far along? Maybe I could take a detour.'

'Sorry, ma'am, but the surface is unstable. I couldn't allow it.' Steel threaded his voice for all his deference.

'I see.' She scanned the wooded hillside. There must be other tracks.

'If I might suggest, ma'am?'

'Yes?'

'There's an easy circuit walk above the castle.'

Tamsin repressed a sigh. She needed more than a tame stroll. This restlessness demanded a better outlet. She'd avoided the squash court in case she met the prince again. Perhaps she should try to work off her excess energy there.

'Thanks. I'll think about it.' She smiled, acknowledging his nod, and turned uphill.

The track curved and she looked back. He was still there, watching, as he spoke into his walkie-talkie.

She shivered. It was nonsense to think he was reporting her movements. Yet the claustrophobic feeling that dogged her intensified. In the archives the new staff meant she was never alone and whenever she left her rooms she seemed to run into staff.

Tamsin paused as the castle came into full view. A thrill sped through her as she took in the circular towers, crenellated battlements and banners fluttering black, blue and gold against the bright sky.

Just the place for tales of romance and derring do. For princes on white chargers rescuing damsels in distress.

Cradled by snow-capped peaks, its grey stone rose sheer from the mountain, high above the dark forest. It had an eagle's eye view down the valley to lands its owners had ruled for generations.

A nineteenth-century fad for gothic architecture had turned the once-grim stronghold into a fairy tale showpiece.

Yet below were grim dungeons where enemies had languished. The prince's word had always been law here and the ruthlessness of Ruvingian princes was legendary. They always got what they wanted.

Shadows moved beneath the portcullis. Tamsin's pulse danced and her breathing shallowed as she recognised the man in the lead: tall, powerfully proportioned and aristocratic with his confident stride and strong features. He matched his home perfectly.

Then it was too late to stand gawking. He'd seen her. He turned and dismissed his staff.

And all she could think of was how it had felt cradled tight in his arms. The intensity of his kiss. The passion that had ravaged her senses and left her craving more.

Every night she'd tossed in her bed, remembering. Imagining things that left her feverish and unsettled. Furiously she tried to repress the blush staining her cheeks, hoping he'd put it down to the chill wind.

'Tamsin.' He stopped a few paces away.

Despite her embarrassment her lips curved in response when he smiled, a dimple grooving his cheek.

She could almost believe he was pleased to see her, though she told herself he didn't really care. She tried to dredge up anger. He'd kissed her out of pity.

'Alaric.' She liked saying his name. Too much. 'How are you? I thought you were away?' Too late she realised she sounded far too interested in his activities.

'Business kept me away until today.' Was that a cloud moving over the sun or had his bright gaze shadowed?

'We need to talk about my work.' She drew herself up straight, reminding herself that was all that mattered. Not her shocking weakness for indigo eyes. 'I haven't been able to access the chronicle to continue my translation. Your staff claim not to know where it is.' Indignation rose that he didn't trust her with her own find!

'My priority is ensuring absolute secrecy till we confirm it's genuine.' His expression grew stern.

Tamsin opened her mouth to protest that it shouldn't stop her work. 'However, arrangements will be made to enable you access while maintaining security.'

'Thank you.' Her indignation fizzled, leaving her feeling wrong-footed.

'Now, would you like to come out with me tonight?'

He sounded like a polite host, entertaining a guest. Except he'd bought her cooperation, bribed her with staff for her project.

The knowledge stopped her pleasure in his smile. The staff had turned up days ago and now it was time to deliver on her part of the bargain.

'Where are we going?' She might as well be gracious about it.

His smile broadened and her lungs squeezed. He really was the most stunning man.

'To a ski resort.' He named a town famous for exclusive luxury that drew the world's most prestigious VIPs. 'There's an event I must take part in then we'll stay for dinner.' No mention of her role as decoy. The man was a diplomat when he wanted to be.

'Fine.' She stepped forward and he turned, shortening his stride to match hers.

'Watch the icy path.' He clasped her elbow and she tensed. Heat rayed from his touch, countering the wintry air.

He held her arm even when they reached safer ground. Tamsin didn't fuss by telling him to release her. He'd think she read too much into the gesture. Hurriedly she searched for something to say.

'What should I wear?'

He slanted her a piercing glance and the air sizzled between them. He was remembering, too.

I don't give a damn about your clothes, he'd said.

And then he'd kissed her.

Tamsin's pulse accelerated painfully as she watched his impassive face. Or had their kiss meant so little he'd forgotten it?

'Some will be in ski gear and the rest dressed for an evening out. Take your pick.' Heat shimmied through her as their gazes collided and she felt again that sensation like chocolate melting, deep inside.

Spending time with Alaric had to be the biggest mistake of her life! Yet despite her doubts, Tamsin couldn't resist the invitation in his smile and the intriguing mystery of his cool, blue eyes.

Even when he annoyed her, Alaric made her feel alive; brimming with an effervescence she'd never known.

* * *

Tamsin stood on the terrace of an exclusive resort hotel, huddled into the soft luxury of the full length faux-fur coat that had been delivered just before she left.

She'd been about to object, uncomfortable with accepting clothes Alaric had bought when she'd seen his note.

To keep you warm tonight. This was my mother's. I'm sure she'd approve its loan.

He'd lent her something of his mother's? Ridiculous to feel such pleasure that he'd trust her with the gorgeous garment. Yet she couldn't dispel delight that he'd thought of her comfort. Without being obvious, he'd also ensured she wouldn't look too out of place in this A-list crowd.

Tamsin glanced at the glamorous, beautiful people surrounding her, some of the faces familiar from press reports. They quaffed vintage champagne as if it were water. And the jewels—even by lamplight some of the women almost blinded her with their casually worn gems.

She stroked the soft coat. For now it didn't matter that beneath its elegant lines she wore a chain store dress and a pair of plain court shoes, her best, which she'd bet none of the sophisticated women here would be seen dead in.

'Here they come!' Excitement rippled through the gathering and Tamsin turned to look up at the blackness of the mountain looming above.

Butterflies danced in her stomach. It was hunger, not excitement at the idea of Alaric joining her.

'There they are.'

Now Tamsin saw it. A flicker of colour high on the mountain. As she watched the flicker became a glow then a tiny jewel-like thread of colour trailing down the slope.

The moon emerged from behind clouds to illuminate the imposing outline of one of Europe's most famous peaks. Its cool brightness intensified the scene's magical quality.

She couldn't take her eyes from the ribbon of rainbow colours descending in swooping curves through the silver gilt night. She'd never seen anything like it. Excited murmurs in a dozen languages buzzed in her ears and she found herself grinning, rapt in the spectacle.

Her spine tingled as a clear chorus of voices rose. A cluster of people, many in traditional Ruvingian costume, waited on a flat area beside the hotel.

The singing stopped and in the silence Tamsin heard the whoosh of skis. The stream of colour descended to the clearing, resolving into dozens of skiers, each holding a coloured lantern in one hand and a basket in the other.

'They skied that slope with no hands?' The mountain was notoriously dangerous.

'It's tradition,' said a woman in cherry red ski clothes and scintillating diamonds. 'Didn't you know?'

Tamsin shook her head, her gaze on the lead skier. Alaric. Her knees gave a little wobble as she took in his proud, handsome face and his easy grace as he slid to a flourishing halt. He handed the basket to a blonde who curtseyed and blushed. Each skier delivered a basket and was rewarded with a goblet.

'Mulled wine,' said the woman beside her.

There was a bustle as Alaric stepped out of his skis and headed purposefully through the crowd. It parted before him and Tamsin wondered what it would be like to have that effect on people.

His progress wasn't entirely easy. Others moved towards him, all women, she noted, frowning.

No wonder he had a reputation as a ladies' man. He didn't even have to search them out!

Some smiled, others greeted him and still others reached out to touch. A twist of something sharp coiled through Tamsin's stomach as she watched a beautiful redhead kiss him on the cheek.

Tamsin's sense of not belonging rushed back full force. Why was she here? Companion indeed! This was a farce.

'Your Highness.' The woman beside her bobbed a curtsey then Tamsin forgot her as she looked up into eyes like midnight. Black hair flopped roguishly on his brow and his lips curved in an intimate smile that sent shivers of longing scudding through her.

'Tamsin.' He lifted the silver goblet in his hand. She had a moment to notice its intricate design, then the scent of spiced wine filled her nostrils and its sweet pungency was in her mouth.

Heat exploded within, surging through her blood. An instant later it exploded again as she watched Alaric lift the goblet to his lips, turning it deliberately to drink from the same place she had. His eyes held hers as he tilted it and drank. Not a sip like hers but a full bodied swallow.

Fire sparked across Tamsin's skin at the blatant sexual message in his eyes. She told herself it was an act.

Yet a crazy part of her wished the message she read in his stare was real. She must be losing her mind!

Seated at a quiet table by a window overlooking the resort, Tamsin tried to relax. It was impossible with Alaric, like a sleek, dark predator, on the other side of the table.

The taste of spiced wine was on her tongue but it was the taste of *him* she remembered. Why couldn't she get that kiss from her mind? Heat flooded her cheeks as she sought for something to say, convinced his brooding eyes read too much of her inner turmoil.

'Tell me about the night ski. Is it an old tradition?'

Alaric settled back in his chair and stretched his legs. Tamsin shifted as they brushed hers.

'Since the seventeenth century. The locals have re-enacted it ever since.'

'Re-enacted what?' Maybe if she focused on this she wouldn't react to his lazy sensuality.

'It was the worst winter on record. Avalanches cut the valley off and crop failure meant the villagers were starving. In desperation some young men set off through near blizzard conditions to get supplies, though everyone believed the trek doomed.' Alaric's voice was as dark and alluring as the rest of him. Tamsin felt it curl around her like the caress of fur on bare skin.

'Fortunately one of the avalanches also brought down rock and opened a new route out of the valley. Weeks later they returned with supplies. Ever since the locals have commemorated the feat, and the salvation of the village.'

'And the wine?' She couldn't shake the idea there'd been hidden significance in the way he'd shared that goblet.

'Just to warm the skiers.' His eyes gleamed.

'That's all?'

He leaned forward, his gaze pinioning her till her only movement was the pulse thudding at her throat.

'You think I've deviously tied you to me in some arcane tradition? That we're betrothed, perhaps?'

Her cheeks grew fiery. 'Of course not!'

His brows arched disbelievingly but she refused to admit how the simple act of sharing his wine had taken on such ridiculous significance in her mind. If only he hadn't looked so sinfully sexy and dangerous as he'd deliberately drunk from her side of the cup.

'Don't fret,' he purred, reaching out to cover her hand in a blatantly possessive gesture. 'Our companionship has a purpose and my actions were designed to achieve that purpose. They succeeded, don't you think?'

'Admirably! Everyone got the message.' She tugged her hand free and placed it in her lap, conscious of the interest emanating from the rest of the restaurant. There were celebrities aplenty here but Alaric was the man drawing every eye.

He raised a glass of delicious local wine in a toast. 'To more success.'

Reluctantly she lifted her glass. 'And a speedy resolution.'

Alaric smiled as he watched her sip the wine. Not the usual practised smile that he'd learned to put on like a shield from an early age. But a smile of genuine pleasure. Tamsin Connors pleased him, and not just because she was refreshing after so many grasping, eager women.

He enjoyed her company, even when she was prickly. And tonight the glow in her cheeks gave her a softness at odds with the strict hairstyle and unimaginative dress.

His silence unnerved her. He saw it in the way she shifted in her seat. Yet he didn't try to ease her tension. If she was on edge she was more likely to reveal her true self. He needed to understand her, find out how far he could trust her.

'You know,' she mused, her eyes not quite meeting his, 'there's a way out of your problem. Fall in love with a nice, suitable princess and marry. Women won't bother you then.'

Instantly Alaric's sense of satisfaction vanished. He stiffened, fingers tightening around the stem of his glass. 'I'm in no hurry to marry. Besides,' he drawled, aiming to cut off this line of conversation, 'the princes of Ruvingia never marry for love.'

For an instant he allowed himself to remember his brother, the only person with whom he'd been close. Love had barely featured in their lives and when it had it had been destructive. Felix had been ecstatic in his delusion that he'd found the love of his life. He'd been doomed to disappointment.

Ruthlessly, Alaric clamped a lid on the acrid memories.

'What about the princesses?'

'Pardon?' Alaric looked up to find Tamsin, far from being abashed by his offhand response, was intrigued.

'Do princesses of Ruvingia ever marry for love?'

'Not if they know what's good for them,' he growled.

The hint of a smile curving her lips died and she sat back, her expression rigid and her eyes wide.

Damn. He felt like he'd kicked a kitten when she looked like that. He speared a hand through his hair and searched for a response that would ease the hurt from her eyes.

'Royal marriages are arranged. It's always been that way.' Until Felix had made the mistake of thinking himself in love.

Love was an illusion that only led to pain.

'Even your parents?' she said wistfully. 'That wasn't a love match?'

Clearly Tamsin Connors had a romantic streak. She'd probably grown up reading about princes rescuing maidens, falling in love and living happily ever after. Obviously she had no idea how far from the truth her fantasy was.

'My parents married because their families arranged a suitable match.'

'I see.' She looked so disappointed he relented.

'I was too young to remember but I'm told my mother was besotted with my father, though it was an arranged match.'

'She died when you were little? I'm sorry.'

Alaric shrugged. You didn't miss what you'd never known. Maternal love was something he'd never experienced.

'It must have been hard for your father, left alone to bring up his family.'

Alaric watched her sharply but she wasn't fishing for details, just expressing genuine sympathy.

'My father had plenty of assistance. Staff. Tutors. You name it.'

Looking back on his boyhood it seemed his remote, irascible father had only appeared in order to deliver cutting lectures about all the ways Alaric failed to live up to his golden-haired brother. For a man who, according to under stairs gossip, had only slept with his wife long enough to conceive a spare heir, he'd been remarkably uninterested in his younger son.

'Still,' she said, 'he must have missed your mother. Even if he didn't marry for love, he would have grown to care for her.'

Alaric shook his head. No point letting her believe some fairy tale when the truth was publicly known. 'My father didn't waste any time finding another woman.'

'He married again?'

'No, he simply ensured there was a willing woman warming his bed whenever he wanted one. He was a good-looking man and he had no trouble attracting women.'

People said Alaric was like him.

Hadn't the disaster with Felix stemmed from Alaric's too-easy success with women?

There was no disputing the fact Alaric, like his father, had never fancied himself in love, possibly because he'd never experienced it. Ice trickled down his spine. Maybe it was a character flaw they shared. That they were incapable of love. Unlike Felix. Unlike Alaric's mother who'd reputedly died of a broken heart.

'I see.'

He doubted it. Tamsin, he was beginning to suspect, had a naïve streak a mile wide.

He'd bet she'd be horrified to learn the first girl to profess love for Alaric had simply been aiming to meet his father. That *love* had been code for sex and expediency in a quest for the power and riches she'd hoped to obtain in the bed of a man old enough to be her own father.

Alaric had learned his lessons early. If there was one thing he'd never be foolish enough to do, it was to give his heart.

CHAPTER SIX

'THANKS for coming, Alaric. It was good to talk before I put the expansion plans to the rest of the board.'

Alaric turned. He didn't let his eyes flicker to the scar disfiguring Peter's cheek and neck. He'd long ago trained himself not to, knowing pity was the last thing his old comrade wanted. But nothing could prevent the sour tang of guilt in his mouth.

'My pleasure.' He forced himself to smile. 'You know I always have time for the youth centre. I just wish there'd been something like it when we were kids.'

Peter shrugged. 'The army saved us both from turning into feral teenagers.'

Alaric thought of his rebellious teens, chafing at his father's aloof authoritarianism and his own sense of uselessness, kicking his heels between royal duties.

'You could be right. Just as well the military is royalty's accepted profession for superfluous second sons.'

'Hardly superfluous.'

Alaric shrugged. It was the truth, but he wasn't interested in discussing his family.

'I like your Tamsin, by the way. A bit different from your usual girlfriends.'

It was on the tip of Alaric's tongue to say she wasn't his, *yet*. 'She is different.' That's why she fascinated him. She was an enigma. Once solved she'd lose her allure and finally he'd get a full night's sleep.

They walked into the large indoor sports hall to find a crowd clustered below the climbing wall. There was no sign of Tamsin. Last time he'd seen her she'd been engrossed in some new computer programme with a couple of lanky youths.

Then he saw her—halfway up the towering wall.

Bemused, he stared. He'd left her without a qualm, seeing her so involved and with his staff to look after her while he attended his meeting. Had she been pressured into scaling the massive wall? The teens often challenged visitors in a test of courage.

'Way to go, Tamsin!' called one of the youths holding the rope that kept her safe.

Alaric strode over, fury pumping in his veins. At them for forcing her into this. At himself for allowing it to happen.

He slammed to a halt as he realised, far from being petrified, she was making steady progress up the wall.

She wore a helmet but her feet were bare and her trousers rolled up, revealing those shapely calves. The harness she wore outlined the lush femininity of her derriere and made his blood pump even faster.

Tamsin moved with the grace of a natural climber. Another metre and she reached the top. Roars of approval erupted, almost obliterating her exultant laughter.

Who'd have thought it? Prim and proper Dr Connors had the makings of a thrill seeker! He watched her climb down.

'That was fantastic,' she called over her shoulder. 'I…' Looking down she saw him. Her foot jerked beneath her.

'I've got you.' Alaric stepped close. 'Let her down.' They obeyed and a moment later she filled his arms.

She was soft and intriguingly curvaceous for such a slim woman. The warm puff of her breath hazed his neck and his grip tightened.

She fitted snugly in his hold, her breast soft temptation against his chest, the sunshine scent of her enticing. His pulse accelerated but he kept his eyes on her flushed face, rather than linger on the pronounced rise and fall of her breasts.

'Thanks. You can put me down.' She sounded delightfully breathless. Free of her glasses, there was nothing to hide the amber glow of awareness in her eyes. Alaric felt he was falling into sunshine.

He had an intense vision of her looking up at him like that, lips parted invitingly, eyes dazed. But in his mind she was sprawled beneath the royal blue canopy of his bed, naked on silk sheets, awaiting his pleasure.

Alaric's breathing grew choppy as he fought the most primitive of physical reactions. His lower body locked solid at the force of abrupt arousal. The sound of applause and excited comment faded as fire ignited his blood.

Tamsin moved, dragging her gaze from his and fumbling at the strap of her helmet. It dropped away before she could stop it and her hair frothed over his arm in a dark cloud.

The scent of wildflowers hit him.

Forget the bedroom. He wanted this woman on sweet alpine grass. He wanted to watch her eyes light to gold as he plunged deep inside and took her to ecstasy.

'Alaric.' Her voice was deliciously throaty. He wanted to hear her calling his name as she climaxed. 'Please…'

Reluctantly he lowered her to her feet. But holding her had cemented his resolve. Amazingly, for those few moments she'd banished the dark shadows. He'd been utterly consumed by sexual need. Just as when they'd kissed.

It was no longer enough to satisfy his pride by making Tamsin Connors beg for his kisses. Alaric craved the release he knew he could find in her sweet, supple body.

And he intended to have it.

'A moment of your time before you go in.'

Tamsin halted at the door to the castle's staff quarters. Slowly she turned, schooling her face to polite interest. They were alone, the security men melting away when they arrived back from the youth centre.

In the late afternoon gloom of the castle courtyard, Alaric's face was unreadable but the way he towered above her, his shoulders blocking her vision, reminded her of the night he'd kissed her.

Of the way it had felt an hour ago when he'd held her in his embrace.

A shiver tingled to her toes as she recalled the heat in his eyes and the answering fire in her belly, and lower, at the message that had passed wordlessly between them.

No! Her imagination ran riot. Prince Alaric would never look at her with desire. Her hormones made her see what wasn't there. He'd played at intimacy for their audience.

'Yes?' At least her voice was steady.

For a moment he simply gazed down. She sensed the intensity of his regard, despite the way his eyelids dropped to half-mast. That gave him a dangerously seductive look that made her pulse race into overdrive.

He leaned closer, his breath tickling her forehead.

'Why wear those glasses? You don't need them.'

Stunned, she stepped back, only to find she'd already backed up against the door. He followed, lifting a hand idly to rest on the wall near her head. Instantly Tamsin was torn between unease at the sense of being trapped and, worse, delight at being so near him.

Beneath her jacket her breasts felt fuller. She wanted his hand there, she realised with a stifled gasp, on her breast, moulding her flesh.

This was worse than anything she'd felt for Patrick. Far worse. Surely it wasn't normal to feel this lick of heat between her legs or the heavy swirl low in her belly?

'Tamsin?'

Flustered, she grappled for the thread of the conversation. 'My glasses?' She touched them, gaining a moment's reassurance from their familiarity. 'For magnification. I do a lot of close work.'

'They don't magnify much.'

How did he know that?

'You don't need them now. You took them off to play squash and to climb. Why not remove them when you're not working?'

'I'm used to them.' Even in her own ears it sounded lame, but it was true. 'I've worn them for years.'

'Then perhaps it's time you came out from behind them.' Alaric leaned forward, his words a whispered caress that tantalised her bare skin.

He lifted a hand and for a moment she thought he was going to grab her glasses. Instead he stroked her hair from her face.

After taking it down to fit under the climbing helmet, she'd only secured it quickly and now strands escaped. She felt them tickle her neck.

Or was that his warm breath? He'd lowered his head and they stood close.

'What difference does it make to you?' Her voice was uneven, as if she'd run up the zigzag road to the castle.

'None.' Again his fingers stroked as he tucked hair behind her ear. Did she imagine his touch lingered? 'I just wondered why you hid behind them.'

Tamsin stiffened. 'I'm not hiding!' She'd acquired the glasses when she'd worked on a particularly difficult manuscript at university. The text had been so tiny she'd suffered eye strain until she'd got them.

She watched one dark eyebrow rise questioningly. She was about to reiterate her words when something stopped her.

The memory of how comfortable she'd felt behind her new glasses. How easy not to notice when older students pointed and dug each other in the ribs as they whispered about her. How hurtful it was when they'd gone to the pub after lectures leaving her, the young kid, behind and alone.

When had she decided to use her glasses all the time? Had it even been a conscious decision?

Or had she slipped into the habit the same way she'd filled her wardrobe with clothes that were functional rather than fashionable? *Because there was no point pretending to be what she wasn't.* Because she was what she was: a brain rather than a face. Known for her intellect, never invited out or pursued for her looks or personality.

Was he right? Had she been hiding? Isolating herself as a defence mechanism?

'Tamsin?'

'Was there anything else…Alaric?' She stood straighter, looking him in the eye, her brain whirling with the implications of his words. She'd think about it later. She couldn't think when he was so close, so…distracting.

'As a matter of fact there is.' He smiled and her heart jerked as if pulled on a string.

Tamsin swallowed, telling herself it was a trick of the fading light that made his expression seem intimate, as if he wanted nothing more than to stand here with her.

'Yes? You have another outing planned?' It didn't matter that she'd enjoyed her afternoon. That she'd revelled in the company of the teenagers, seemingly antisocial and yet so enthusiastic. Alaric had only invited her to be seen with him. Because she was a decoy.

He must have been ecstatic when she'd swooned in his arms, reinforcing their fictional relationship. Heat rocketed to her cheeks at the memory.

Would he be angry or amused if he realised how she felt about him? That the thought of him touching her made her long for things far beyond her experience?

'Not an outing.' He paused. 'I'm hosting a winter ball. It's an important event on the calendar.'

'*Another* ball? But you just had one!'

His mouth lifted in a lazy smile that softened her sinews and made her slump, grateful for the solid door behind her. In the gathering dusk Tamsin read the amused glitter in his eyes.

'How puritanical you sound. Do you disapprove?'

'It just seems a little…'

'Excessive?' He shrugged. 'Last week's was a small affair, only eighty or so guests to meet a new consul. The winter ball is something different. In four hundred years it's been held as regular as clockwork every year but one.'

'During war?'

Alaric's expression sobered. 'No.' Tamsin waited what seemed a full minute before he continued. 'There was no winter ball the year my brother died suddenly.'

Tamsin's flesh chilled as his words, sharp as shattered crystal, scored her.

'I'm sorry, Alaric. So sorry for your loss.' When he'd spoken briefly of his family the other night she'd had the impression they weren't close. Except his brother. The way Alaric spoke of him she sensed a special bond there.

She lifted her hand to reach for him, then dropped it. He wouldn't welcome her touch. He'd never looked so remote.

'Thank you.' He nodded curtly. 'But the point is this event, above all, is one where I'd be grateful for your presence.'

'Of course.'

It didn't matter that attending a ball was the last thing she wanted, that she'd be way out of her comfort zone. She'd seen the pain behind Alaric's cool expression. For a moment she'd seen anguish shadow his eyes and the sight hit her a body blow.

If he wanted her, she'd be there.

She didn't pause to question her decision.

'Good. Thank you.' His lips tilted in a ghost of his usual smile and something seemed to unravel, deep inside her. 'A dresser will attend you tomorrow and you can make your selection to wear to the ball.'

'But I—'

'Let me guess.' This time his smile was real and her heart tumbled. *Oh, she had it bad.* 'You're going to insist on buying your gown?'

'Well, yes.'

'You'd only buy a ball gown as a favour to me.' He stroked a finger down Tamsin's cheek, effectively stifling the objection rising in her throat. That simple caress held her still, breathless with pleasure.

'Consider it a work-related expense. I need you there and you need a dress. Unless you have one with you?'

Tamsin shook her head. She'd never owned a ball gown.

He leaned in. For a heart-stopping moment she wondered if he'd kiss her. She should object but her willpower seeped away. Her damp palms spread on the door behind her for support and her pulse juddered madly against her ribcage.

'Leave it to me.' His lips were so close Tamsin almost felt them against her skin. She sucked in a difficult breath as he spoke again in that deep, seductive whisper.

'All you have to do is relax and enjoy.'

CHAPTER SEVEN

TAMSIN lifted a hand to her hair then changed her mind and let it fall. She didn't want to disturb the softly elegant knot with its glittering pins or the artfully loose tendrils caressing her neck.

The dresser who'd returned this evening had done far more than zip up the dress. She'd transformed Tamsin into a woman she barely recognised. A woman who looked attractive in a way Tamsin never had before.

At first she'd thought it was simply the ball gown that made the difference. Of red silk shot with amber and gold, it was unlike anything she'd owned. From the moment she'd put it on she'd felt…special. The last of her scruples about accepting it disintegrated as she twirled before the mirror.

The bodice, cut high and straight above her breasts to leave her shoulders bare, made her look feminine and elegant. Even the fact that she'd had to go braless, relying on the dress's hidden support in lieu of a strapless bra she didn't own, didn't dampen her excitement.

It was shallow of her to feel wonderful because she looked good. But Tamsin didn't care. It was such a novel experience! Excitement bubbled in her veins. She felt she could take on the world!

For weeks Tamsin had featured in newspaper and magazine articles beside Alaric. Worst of all, the ones that made her cringe, were the 'then and now' pieces. Showing Alaric with previous girlfriends, all gorgeous and sophisticated. Those photos were set against pictures of Tamsin, looking anything but chic, her expression startled or, worse, besotted as she stared up at the powerful man beside her.

She wasn't besotted. She wouldn't let herself be.

The theme of each article had been the same. What did Alaric see in her? Those pictures had confirmed every doubt she'd harboured about herself, especially since Patrick.

More than once she'd been tempted to call a halt to this charade. She didn't, not simply because she'd given her word, but because being with Alaric, the focus of his glowing looks, made her feel good.

Even it if was a sham, she *enjoyed* being with him. It was balm to her wounded soul. Was it so wrong to enjoy the pretence that he genuinely liked her?

Yet the temptation was dangerous.

Now for the first time Tamsin knew she looked like a prince's companion. Delight filled her that this time there'd be no snide conjecture, no damning photos. This time she looked… attractive.

Tonight she'd learned so much. Things she'd always told herself she was too busy to bother with. Things her mother, so profoundly uninterested in fashion, hadn't thought to teach her. Like what shade of eye shadow accentuated the colour of Tamsin's eyes without being too obvious. Like how to tame her hair into a sophisticated style.

Yet the dresser said it was the glow in Tamsin's skin, the sparkle in her eyes that made her look so good tonight.

Surely that had been a pep talk to give her confidence. Apart from the clothes and light make-up, she was the same. As she turned before the mirror, feeling the silk swirl around her legs, Tamsin experienced a prickle of unease. The colour in her cheeks was because of the dress, that's all.

For there was only one other possible explanation. That her inner sparkle was anticipation at the idea of spending the evening with Alaric, maybe even dancing in his arms.

She stopped abruptly, letting her long skirts settle around her. No! She wouldn't let it be so. To Alaric she was a convenient companion. She wouldn't spin fantasies about him. These past weeks as his companion had been surprisingly delightful. She enjoyed his company. *But that's all.*

The phone rang and she snatched it up, grateful for the interruption to her disturbing thoughts.

'Tamsin? How are you, darling?'

Instantly her spine stiffened. She'd hoped not to hear that voice again for a long, long time. She'd crossed Europe to avoid this man. To pull herself together after he'd hurt her so badly. Now he had the temerity to call her darling!

'Who is this?'

'Ah, sweetheart, it's Patrick of course. Are you still upset about the way we parted?' He paused as if waiting for her to speak. 'Didn't I apologise?'

He'd apologised all right, while smirking at his success and her gullibility in believing he could ever interest himself in a plain Jane like her! As apologies went it had been a masterpiece of form over sentiment. He hadn't been sorry and in that moment Tamsin had finally realised how blind she'd been to his true personality.

In love with the idea of love, she'd fallen for him like a ripe peach. Or from his perspective, like a dried up prune! Too late she'd discovered his taste really ran to curvy blondes who dressed to reveal rather than conceal.

'It's late for a business call.' She was proud of her nonchalant tone.

'You're assuming it's business?'

'What do you want, Patrick?' He thought he was God's gift to women but he surely couldn't believe her weak enough to care for him after what he'd done.

His sigh might have moved her once but now she merely felt a burst of impatience.

It was only when he mentioned the date testing on the sample she'd sent to her home institution that Tamsin grew interested. By the time he'd finished speaking her scalp prickled with excitement.

She'd *known* this was special! Now the dating proved it.

Yet doubt lingered. On the face of it she now had proof that Alaric should be Maritz's next king. But caution warned her to make absolutely sure. Just because the document's age was right didn't prove the content.

Besides, Alaric wasn't as eager as she'd expected. Did he really not want to be king? Look at the strict security he'd instituted around the chronicle. It was locked away the minute she'd finished work each day.

'Tamsin? Are you still there?'

'Of course. I'll look forward to reading the report when you email it. Thanks for calling.'

'I said it seems you've got an interesting cache of documents. I hear on the grapevine the prince himself gave you extra staff for the project. Plus old Schillinger says you've sent him copies of some fascinating pages.'

'That's right.' She frowned. There was no way Patrick or anyone else could guess the explosive revelations in the manuscript. Those pages were kept here under lock and key. Dr Schillinger's interest in the rest was purely linguistic.

'Perhaps if it's such a find you'd feel better with another expert there. Someone you know you can work with.' He paused as if waiting for her to speak. 'I have a lot on at the moment but for you'd I'd tear myself away and...'

'No! That's not necessary.'

Did he think she was still so besotted that she'd invite him here after the way he'd treated her? Had she really been such a pushover?

'Tamsin.' His voice deepened to a cajoling note. 'I hurt you and I've regretted it ever since. I made a mistake and I'm not too proud to admit it. If I came over there we could pick up where we left off. I'm worried for you. Sometimes on the rebound people behave impulsively.'

Was he referring to the press reports linking her and Alaric? He had a hide!

How had she fallen for his oily charm? The only person Patrick cared about was Patrick. It made her sick to realise she'd been so needy she'd let him walk all over her without seeing his selfish opportunism.

As for his wet kisses and perfunctory embraces... Tamsin shuddered. How had she ever thought him appealing?

She remembered Alaric's demanding, exciting kiss. The combustible heat that consumed them and made her feel like she soared close to the sun.

In comparison Patrick's pallid caresses faded to insignificance. Now so did he: a mean, conniving man who wasn't worth her time or emotional energy.

'No, Patrick. I appreciate your offer to *tear yourself away.*' Her lips curled at his attempt to muscle in on what he thought was a project to further his career. 'It's all under control. The staff are excellent and we've gelled into a great team. Of course, if ever we need further support I'll be sure to let you know.' *When hell froze over.*

'But I—'

'Sorry, Patrick. I can't talk. I have to go.'

She put down the phone then stroked unsteady hands along the soft fabric of her dress, trying to conjure again her earlier pleasure.

Her stomach churned from hearing his voice. Not because she missed him, but at the knowledge of how close she'd come to making a complete fool of herself. She'd once considered *giving* herself to that…toad of a man!

Tamsin was fed up with being second best. Being *used.*

First Patrick and now Alaric, who only wanted her as a decoy. It didn't matter that Alaric also made her feel exciting, dangerous, unfamiliar things. That he brought her to tingling life like a sleeper waking from long slumber.

She was tired of being manipulated by men who wanted her for their schemes. Men who saw her as a convenience to be exploited.

Not a real woman of flesh and blood and feelings.

She stared in the mirror, taking in the reflection of a woman who was her and yet not her. Same nose, same eyes, same person, but so different from the old Tamsin everyone took for granted.

She was tired of hiding. Of not being noticed as a woman.

The idea of leaving the protective comfort of her usual role, of daring to pretend to be feminine and desirable, filled her with trepidation. Yet Alaric was right. Tamsin had isolated herself.

She owed it to herself not to hide behind her work and her past any longer. She might be out of her depth tonight but she was no coward.

Deliberately she lifted her hand and removed her glasses, dropping them onto a nearby table. Straightening her shoulders she left the room, her head high.

Alaric viewed formal balls as a necessary evil. Until he turned from greeting an ambassador and her husband to see the next guest in line and the air punched from his lungs.

She was breathtaking.

Among the bejewelled and bedecked glitterati she was unadorned, yet she glowed with a radiance that set her apart. She didn't need diamonds and platinum. Her skin was flawless, her lips a glossy pout that turned his blood molten hot with instant hunger. Her dark hair was a sensuous invitation to touch. It looked like she'd just pinned it up after rising from a bath or bed. As if it would tumble down at any moment around her bare shoulders.

And her eyes. She'd removed the glasses and her amber-gold eyes were even more vibrant, more beautiful than he remembered. They blazed with an expression he'd never seen.

He'd *known* she was hiding her real self. But nothing had prepared him for this.

The ambassador moved away and Tamsin approached.

Alaric stiffened. She was fully covered, more fully than many of the women present. Yet he knew an almost overpowering impulse to unbutton his military tunic and toss it around her bare shoulders.

He didn't miss the arrested glances from the men nearby. He wanted to growl out a warning to keep their distance. To look away.

'Tamsin.' His voice worked, though it emerged brusquely from frozen vocal cords. 'It's good to see you.' If his muscles weren't so stiff with shock he'd have laughed at the enormity of that understatement. He bowed over her hand, resorting to punctilious formality to prevent himself shepherding her straight out the way she'd come. Away from those admiring stares.

His gaze dropped to her bodice, tightly fitted to show off her slim frame and full breasts. Flaring skirts accentuated Tamsin's narrow waist and for an insane moment he found himself distracted, musing whether he could span her with his hands.

'Hello, Alaric.' Her voice was low and throaty, yanking his libido into roaring life.

His hand tightened around hers and he wondered what would happen if he swept her away right now and didn't come back. He was within an ace of scandalising everyone, had moved closer, when she spoke again.

'I'm sorry I'm late.'

Reluctantly he dropped her hand and stepped back, removing himself from temptation.

'You're not late at all.' His voice was unnaturally clipped. 'Please, go on in. I'll join you soon.'

She nodded and he turned away, forcing himself to greet the next guests in the reception line. Never had it been so hard to focus on duty.

It was easier than she'd expected to mingle at a royal ball. Tamsin smiled as she sipped a glass of champagne and listened to the conversation around her.

'You're enjoying yourself?' asked Peter, the friendly community centre coordinator she'd met just over a week ago.

'How could I not? I've met so many fascinating people and I love dancing.' She'd only discovered that tonight, as partner after partner had whirled her round the mirrored ballroom, her dress swishing about her and her blood singing in her veins. It had been heady and delightful.

She turned. Peter wore an officer's dress uniform. The gold braid and the neat row of medals across his chest gleamed in the light of the chandeliers. He looked the model of a dashing soldier of a couple of centuries ago, except for the scar on his neck and cheek.

He laughed. 'It's true, then, that all the girls love a uniform.'

'Sorry. Was I staring?' His smile dispelled any embarrassment. 'It's just so unusual. Uniforms have changed since the Napoleonic Wars.'

'Not in Ruvingia. Not for formal occasions.' He winked. 'Especially as they make us so popular with the ladies. But in the field we wear khakis like everyone else.'

A pair of dancers swung by: Alaric looking like he'd stepped from the pages of a fairy tale in a uniform like Peter's only with more medals pinned to his chest, and in his arms a delicate blonde woman glittering in azure silk and sapphires.

Something struck Tamsin in the ribs. Jealousy? The possibility appalled her.

Despite promising to join her hours ago, Alaric had only danced with her once. He'd held her at arm's length, propelling her around the floor as if she were an elderly maiden aunt. Not close in his embrace as he smiled down into her face like he did with the gorgeous blonde.

The pain in her ribs twisted, intensifying.

'The prince, too? Surely he doesn't have to wear khaki?'

'Alaric? You don't know—?'

The surprise in Peter's voice made her swing round to meet his suddenly sombre face.

'Don't know what?'

He shrugged and she had the impression he was buying time before answering. The instinct she'd always trusted with her work sent a tiny shiver down her backbone.

'You mean Alaric is a real soldier, too?' If Peter was surprised by her use of the prince's first name he didn't show it. 'I thought the uniform might be a perk of position. Like being a royal sponsor rather than a member of the regiment.'

Yet even as Tamsin spoke she recalled her first impression of Alaric. His controlled power and athleticism proclaimed him a man of action, not a tame administrator.

'Some perk!' Peter shook his head. 'He won his commission through talent and hard work. Much good it did him.'

Tamsin put her glass down. 'What do you mean?' Peter's grim expression spiked foreboding through her.

'There was nothing pretend about our work. Alaric was our commanding officer and a good one, too. But with command comes a sense of responsibility. That can weigh heavily on a man who genuinely cares, especially when things go wrong.'

He half lifted his hand towards his scarred face and Tamsin's heart squeezed in sympathy. She wished she'd never started this conversation.

'I'm sorry,' she said breathlessly. 'I shouldn't have brought it up.'

He smiled. 'Because of this?' He gestured to his face. 'Don't be. There are worse things, believe me.' He looked at the dance floor as Alaric and his partner swung by again. 'Not all scars are on the outside, you know. At least mine have healed.'

Tamsin's gaze followed the prince. So handsome, so powerful, standing out effortlessly from every other man here. The focus of so many longing female glances.

Yet Peter hinted at hidden scars. Could he be right?

She thought of the way Alaric's shadowed eyes belied his easy charm, hinting at dark secrets.

Out of nowhere came the recollection of Alaric's ashen face after he'd saved that boy from serious burns. The prince's expression had been stark with pain or shock. He'd frozen rigid, eyes staring blankly as if looking at something distant that horrified yet held him in thrall.

'Tamsin?'

'Sorry?' She turned to find Peter holding out his hand.

'Would you like to waltz?'

She met his friendly dark eyes and tore her thoughts from the man even now bowing to some aristocratic lady on the other side of the ballroom.

She spent far too much time fretting about Alaric.

'I'd love to.'

For the next hour she danced with partner after partner, revelling in the exquisite venue, the glamorous crowd, the pleasure of the dance. Resolutely she tried not to notice Alaric dancing with every pretty woman in the room. Finally, pleading exhaustion, she let her partner lead her to a relatively quiet corner for champagne and conversation.

He was an editor from a national newspaper, good looking and full of entertaining stories that made her laugh. Tamsin saw the openly admiring light in his eyes and felt a warm glow inside. Here was one man at least who didn't look on her as second best!

Plus he was flatteringly interested in her work, suggesting a feature article on the archives and preservation work.

'May I interrupt?'

At the sound of that deep voice her companion halted in mid-sentence. 'Your Highness, of course.'

Reluctantly Tamsin turned. She'd told herself she was glad Alaric hadn't shown her off as his fake companion tonight. She'd wanted to be her own woman, hadn't she?

Yet his lack of interest stung.

Had he finally decided she wasn't up to the job?

Piercing indigo eyes met hers and heat sizzled through her, making the hairs on her arms stand up as if he'd brushed finger-tips along her bare skin.

She searched for the shadows she'd seen in his gaze once before, the shadows Peter had hinted at, but there was nothing wounded about this man. If anything there was a hint of steel in his stare, a tautness about his mouth. He was commanding, assured, supremely confident.

He bowed. The epitome of royal hauteur from his severely combed hair to his mirror polished shoes.

'Tamsin, I believe this is our dance.'

She tried to tell herself she didn't care that he'd come to her at last, but her heart gave a little jump.

'I'll be in contact later, Tamsin.' Her companion smiled and took her wineglass, urging her forward. She had no excuse but to go with Alaric.

A strong hand closed around hers and her heart hammered. Ridiculous! She'd danced with the prince earlier. But then he'd barely looked at her, his formality quenching her excitement.

Now his gaze pinioned her, so intent it smouldered.

What had she done to antagonise him?

'You've made a new friend,' he murmured as he curled long fingers around her waist. His touch evoked a tremor of primitive anxiety. As if she'd stepped too close to a slumbering predator.

Taking a deep breath Tamsin placed an arm on his shoulder, let him clasp her other hand and fixed her gaze on his collar. This was just a dance. For show.

'Yes, several. Everyone's been very pleasant.' Despite the heat flooding her veins as Alaric guided her on the floor, something in his tone chilled her.

'So I saw. You've flitted from man to man all evening.' His voice was harsh and she raised surprised eyes to his. Blue fire flashed like lightning in an approaching storm.

'Your instructions were just that I attend the ball.' Her breasts rose in indignation, straining at the taut fabric of her bodice. 'I hadn't realised I wasn't allowed to mingle.' After ignoring her most of the night, how dare he complain she'd socialised with the other guests?

'Is that what you call it?' He spun her faster till the room whirled around them. Yet in his firm hold Tamsin felt only a heady rush of excitement. As if she were on the edge of something dangerous that nevertheless called to her.

'Do you have a problem, Alaric?' She told herself she was breathless because of the speed with which they circled the room. Her skirts belled out around her and her breath shallowed but she didn't feel nervous. She felt…exhilarated.

'Of course not. Why should I?' He kept his gaze fixed over her shoulder. 'Though I'd be sorry to see you hurt.'

'Hurt?' The music ended and they spun to a halt, yet Alaric didn't let her go. They stood in the centre of the dance floor, his grip holding her still.

'We Ruvingians are hospitable to guests. I wouldn't want you to misunderstand and interpret friendliness for something more.'

Tamsin's breath hissed between her teeth as pain lanced her. 'What are you insinuating? That no one would normally want to spend time with a woman like me? That I'm too uninteresting? Or perhaps I'm too plain?'

All the pleasure she'd felt in the evening shattered in that moment, like fragile crystal smashed underfoot. She told herself she didn't believe him, but suddenly the brilliant glare of the antique chandeliers seemed to flicker and dim. The heady excitement of the evening faded to something tawdry and shallow.

She stepped back to break his hold but his grip tightened.

'Of course not. You're misinterpreting my words.'

The music struck up again and around them couples took to the floor, a throng of glittering, designer clad, beautiful people.

She didn't belong here.

'You can let me go, *Your Highness*. You've done your duty dance.' She primmed her lips rather than say any more.

He didn't move, though she saw his chest rise as he took a huge breath.

'I said—'

He muttered something savage under his breath in the local dialect. Something she had no hope of understanding. A second later he pulled her close and twirled her round into the dancing crowd.

This time there was nothing prim or proper about the way they moved. Gone was the staid distance between them. Instead Tamsin was plastered to Alaric's torso. His arm at her waist didn't steady her, it welded her to him. His breath feathered her forehead. His hard thighs cradled her then shifted provocatively between her legs as they danced, evoking a strange hollow ache in her womb.

This close she felt his every movement, partly because her hands were trapped against his chest. His heart pounded fast and strong beneath her palm and despite her anger and hurt, spiralling excitement rose.

'I've had enough dancing,' she gasped as he swung her round and back down the long ballroom. This was too much, too dangerous.

'Nonsense. You love to dance. I've seen the smile on your face all night.'

All night? That implied he'd watched her which he hadn't. He'd been too busy squiring so many socialites onto the floor or engaging them in close conversation.

'You may find it hard to believe, Your Highness, but not all women long to dance with you.' The room flashed by and her heart pounded faster and faster. 'I want to stop.'

'I told you to call me Alaric.'

His body moved against hers and she bit her lip at the surge of pleasure she felt. At the powerful throb building inside. She was pathetic. This was just a dance and with a man she assured herself she didn't like. Though as his arm dropped low on her back, pulling her even tighter, it felt like something altogether different.

'Alaric.' The word was barely audible. Whether from the pulse pounding in her ears or because she couldn't seem to catch her breath, she didn't know.

'That's better.' His voice was rough as his lips moved against her hair. 'I like it when you say my name.'

With one final turn he spun them off the dance floor. Before Tamsin could catch her breath he'd shoved aside a hanging tapestry and hustled her through a door into a narrow passage. A few steps on and another arched door opened on their left. They were through it and in a dimly lit chamber before Tamsin could get her bearings.

A key scraped in the lock, loud as the thrum of her heartbeat. Then she felt a solid wall behind her and Alaric's powerful body trapping her against it.

'What do you think you're doing?' It was meant to sound outraged. Instead Tamsin's voice was uneven, weak with the force of conflicting emotions.

She should abhor this forced intimacy, the press of his body. Yet a secret thrill of pleasure ripped through her.

'Getting you to myself.' Alaric cupped her face in warm palms and lifted her chin so she looked deep into eyes the colour of a stormy night sky. 'I spoiled your evening. I didn't mean to.'

He leaned forward, touching his forehead to hers, hands tunnelling her hair, sending threads of shivery sensation down her spine and across her shoulders. Suddenly it wasn't him holding her prisoner, but her body's response.

'Why?' she croaked, her mouth too dry for speech. How had they come to this?

She should move but she made no resistance as he caressed her scalp and rubbed his nose against hers.

Where was her anger? A deep shuddering sigh rose and she strove to stifle it.

'Because I was jealous.' Shock slammed into her. Yet she felt the words as well as heard them as his lips caressed her eyelids. He really had said it. 'From the moment you appeared tonight I wanted you with me. Only me.'

This couldn't be. Tamsin shook her head, or tried to. He held her so close she couldn't move.

'I don't understand.' She hated her shaky tone but she was at a loss. 'You avoided me most of the night.'

'Displacement activity. I either spent the evening glued to you, or I kept my distance, acting the polite host. There was no happy medium. In the circumstances I thought my self-control admirable.'

His hands moved, slid down her throat and spread across her bare shoulders. Something about his powerful hands touching her so tenderly made her breath catch. His palms circled back to her throat, warming her skin and making her pulse race.

'Every time I saw you smiling at a dance partner I wanted it to be me you smiled at. No one else. Do you have any idea how gorgeous you are tonight?'

He couldn't be serious!

She couldn't think logically when he caressed her like that. She needed to think, to understand.

'Please. Alaric, I…'

'Yes, let me please you. Like this?'

His hands dropped, skimming the silk of her bodice, down the sides of her breasts, till her nipples tightened and the breath seared from her lungs.

Logic didn't matter when his mouth was a mere inch away. She craved him with every fibre of her yearning, untried body. As if this were what she'd secretly waited for. Without volition she raised her face, hungry beyond rational thought for his passion.

His mouth hovered, a breath away from hers.

'I promised I wouldn't.' His husky voice stroked like suede, dragging at her senses. 'So ask me to kiss you, Tamsin.'

CHAPTER EIGHT

ALARIC'S heart slammed against his ribs as he awaited her response. Every nerve, every sinew strained at the need for control.

Part of him was furious that somehow, without him knowing how, she'd cracked the wall he'd built around himself. The wall he'd reinforced the day he'd learnt the need to keep his affairs short and uncomplicated by emotion.

Surely he knew the dangers of reckless affairs!

But this was different.

More than dalliance to hold other women at bay. Far more than a ruse to keep an eye on someone who might, though it surely wasn't possible, be in league with those wanting to undermine the government.

This was an urgent, blood deep hunger.

Somewhere in the ballroom he'd crossed an unseen boundary.

Had it been when he bundled her from the room in full view of scandalised eyes? Or when he'd hauled her close in contravention of every protocol, staking his unmistakeable claim on her? No, it had been earlier. When he'd read the shattered hurt dulling her eyes and known himself the cause. His pain then had been as sharp as any physical wound.

He'd never felt this intensely about a woman.

He didn't *want* emotion. He didn't *want* to feel. Emotions were dangerous, deceitful. Yet for now he functioned on a more primitive level. Raw instinct not reason drove him.

He inhaled deeply, intoxicated by the scent of her. Unthinking, he bent to the delicate curve where her shoulder met her throat, nuzzling flesh so soft it made him feel like a barbarian, demanding her acquiescence.

But he didn't care. Desperation smoked off his skin, clamoured in his pulse, clenched his belly.

From the moment she'd arrived, a demure siren among a crowd of overdressed mannequins, he'd hungered for her.

As he'd watched her laugh and whisper and dance with all those other men he'd experienced a completely alien sensation. A roiling, dangerous, possessive anger.

Jealousy.

The sight of her with that journalist, known as much for his feminine conquests as his provocative editorials, had been a red rag to a bull.

Alaric told himself he'd acted to break up any potential leak of sensitive information. They'd looked like conspirators, their heads close together, their voices lowered. The last thing he wanted was news of her theories about his inheritance splashed across the newspapers.

But in truth he'd stalked across to claim her because he couldn't bear to watch their intimate *tête à tête.*

He laved her skin with his tongue, filling his mouth with her essence. Tamsin shuddered against his hardening body and he did it again, unable to stop. She was delicious.

'Alaric!' Fleetingly he registered her trembling sigh was probably a protest, though it sounded more like encouragement.

'Mmm? I'm not kissing you.' His mouth moved on her skin, trailing up to just below her ear. 'This isn't a kiss.'

He closed his teeth on her lobe in a gentle, grinding bite that made her spasm and fall further into him. Fire flickered through his veins.

So responsive. So incredibly attuned to every caress.

Escalating desire bunched each muscle into lockdown. The press of her belly against his erection was exquisite torture. If she moved again…

'Alaric. No.' It was a throaty whisper that incited rather than protested.

This time he grazed his teeth against the tender flesh below her ear and was rewarded with a shuddering sigh as her head lolled back against the wall. She'd stopped trying to push him away, her fingers curling instead into his tunic as if to draw him closer.

He nipped his way down her throat, revelling in the sinuous slide of her body against his. Unable to resist any longer, he levered away a fraction so he could cup her breasts. High, ripe, lush, they fitted his palms perfectly.

Suddenly slim hands bracketed his jaw, urgently dragging his face up. An instant later Tamsin's lips met his, hard and frantic, delightfully clumsy in her ardour.

When her tongue invaded his mouth it was Alaric's turn to groan at the sheer intensity of sensation. She kissed like a sexy angel. Half seductress, half innocent. For a moment the illusion hovered that she'd saved herself for him alone. That he was her first, her only.

Then he sank into bliss as their tongues slid and mated and thought became impossible. She melded to him with a supple sensuality that drove him to the edge.

He caressed her nipples and she growled in the back of her throat, a decadent purr of pleasure that had him thrusting his knee between hers, parting her legs. In response she arched into his hands, pressing as if she too couldn't get enough.

He needed her. *Now.*

Tearing himself from her grasp he looked down. The gown's neckline was high across her breasts, and tight enough to make them inaccessible. But locating the fastening at the back was the work of a moment. As was lowering the zip enough to loosen the bodice.

He heard her suck in her breath but she didn't protest. Seconds later he peeled the bodice down enough to reveal her cleavage. Her breasts rose and fell rapidly, silently inviting.

With a swift yank of the silky fabric he bared her breasts, watching blush pink nipples bud in the cold air. Not even a strapless bra. Who'd have thought it of prim and proper Dr Connors?

Alaric wasn't complaining. He drank in the sight of pure white skin, full breasts, perfectly formed and deliciously uptilted as if begging for his attention.

His erection pulsed and he almost groaned aloud when she rocked her hips, her thighs widening suggestively. He needed that pelvis to pelvis contact, was desperate to sheath himself inside her. But first…

He lowered his head to her breast, skimmed a caress across her nipple and felt her hands claw his shoulders as if she could no longer stand without support.

He smiled as he kissed the impossibly soft skin around her aureole, revelling in her responsiveness as she gasped and shifted beneath his ministrations.

'Stop teasing.' Her voice was hoarse and uneven. Alaric looked up to see her brow furrow as she watched him. 'Just…' She paused and swallowed hard. 'Do it.'

Despite the wobbly order, Tamsin's eyes were dazed and her skin flushed with arousal. The combination of prim command, desperation and luscious wanton was delicious.

Eyes holding hers, he covered one nipple with his lips, enjoying the way her eyes widened as she watched him draw her into his mouth. Heat shot through him, catapulting him into a world of sensual pleasure as he devoured her sweetness. He sucked hard and she jerked like a puppet on a string, head and neck arched against the wood panelling. Her lower body moved restlessly against him, mimicking his own edgy need to thrust into her.

Not yet. Tamsin was pure delight. He couldn't get enough of her.

He moved to her other breast, daring a tiny erotic bite. She keened her pleasure, her body stiffening around his as if he'd generated an electric current. He breathed deep the sweet scent of feminine arousal and his blood surged south.

She was so hyper-sensitive, was it possible he could bring her to orgasm like this? The notion was almost too much for his threadbare self-discipline.

Another graze of his teeth, this time at her nipple, and another jolt ripped through her. Hungrily he suckled, feeding the demon inside that demanded more, demanded everything from her.

Fumbling, he scrabbled at her skirts, the slippery fabric sliding through his unsteady hands.

He couldn't wait any longer.

Rising, he plastered his mouth over hers, revelling in her kisses as finally his questing fingers found silk clad thighs. Stockings! He found the upper edge, the line where material met bare, smooth flesh and he faltered, heart pounding at the image his mind conjured.

He wanted to spread her on a bed and leisurely inspect the sexy picture she'd make before taking his fill. But he didn't have time, his need was too urgent. His erection throbbed so needily he wondered if he'd be able to get out of his trousers without injury.

He drove her head back with hungry kisses as he hiked her skirts. In a perfect world she wouldn't be wearing panties.

But this was no fantasy. His hands encountered cotton. Despite the sexy gown and stockings, Tamsin had chosen no-nonsense underwear. Underwear damp with arousal.

Spreading his hand to cup her mound, feeling her push hard into his grip, Alaric decided cotton panties were far sexier than silk, more of a turn on than Lycra or lace. Tamsin didn't need frills. She was potently, earthily sexy.

Her hand insinuated itself between their bodies to grapple with the fastening of his dress trousers.

She'd send him over the edge in a moment. He clamped an iron hand round her wrist.

'Don't!' he growled, his voice thick. He forced her hand back, high against the wall and kissed her again. He wanted this to last more than ten seconds. He'd bring her to climax, enjoy watching her take pleasure at his hands, and only then find release in her body.

His fingers slipped beneath cotton, drawn by her heat.

A roaring explosion cracked the night sky, penetrating his fog of sensual arousal. He stiffened, muscles freezing at what sounded like artillery fire. Dread engulfed him as adrenaline spiked in his blood.

By the time the second reverberating boom rent the air he'd opened his eyes and registered the flash of coloured light. Relief surged so strongly he felt weak.

Reality buffeted him and he dropped his head, gasping, trying to force down raw, conflicting emotions. Relief that he was no longer in the nightmare world of armed conflict. And lust—the almost insuperable need for completion. If only willpower could shift blood from his groin to his brain! Never had he so completely lost control.

'What is it?' Tamsin sounded as shaken as he.

Another couple of minutes and he'd have had her, ankles locked round his waist while he shuddered his climax into her. Even now he craved it. The effort of not taking her made him tremble all over.

If he did her gown would be rumpled and stained, proclaiming exactly what they'd been doing.

There'd be stares and rolled eyes about his behaviour but that was nothing. His shoulders were broad, his reputation bad and people's expectations low.

For Tamsin the gossip would be infinitely worse. He couldn't do that to her.

He'd failed Felix. Failed his men. But in this at least surely he could manage to do the right thing.

'Fireworks,' he murmured, his voice a strained whisper. He cleared his throat and released her hand, letting it slide down the wall. 'At the end of the ball we have fireworks and champagne. And a royal toast.'

He had to go. There was no chance to lose himself in Tamsin's slick, warm heat, no matter how much he craved her. Reluctantly he dragged his other hand from between her legs, felt her shudder at the movement and wished it could be different.

He let her skirts fall and stepped away, face drawing tight at the fierce pain in his groin. Desire and guilt and fury at the depth of his own need warred within him. He'd always enjoyed women but this…this was uncharted territory.

'Turn around.' The words emerged brusquely through gritted teeth. She stared up, her lips bruised to plumpness and eyes glazed, then she turned, her head bowed.

He stared at that expanse of naked back, the vulnerable line of her nape, and almost surrendered to temptation again. But a burst of green fire outside the window brought him back to the real world. To duty.

It took him a full minute to do up her dress, his hands were so uncoordinated. When it was done he moved away, wincing at each stiff-legged step as he paced to the window. He needed time before he made a public appearance. He needed to keep away from her before his resolve shattered.

'I'll have to go. I'm expected and my absence will cause speculation.'

He raised his hand to smooth his hair and caught the heady scent of her essence on his fingers. He dropped his hand, summoning every vestige of strength not to go to her when his body screamed out for completion. For Tamsin.

'Of course. I understand.' Her voice sounded flat, but then he couldn't hear clearly over his throbbing pulse and the crack of fireworks.

'Will you be all right?' Still he didn't turn around but stood silhouetted at the arched window, his back to her.

Why wouldn't he look at her?

She was the one embarrassed. He was the playboy with a reputation for loving then leaving each new mistress.

He'd known exactly what he was doing.

'I'm fine,' she murmured, wondering if the lie sounded believable. She was bereft, desperate for a look, a touch, *something*.

Tamsin shivered and slumped against the wall, hands splaying for support as she recalled how expert he'd been.

Her pulse raced out of control as she remembered his knowing, half-lidded look, watching her as he'd sucked at her breast. She squeezed her thighs together at the liquid heat between her legs. Who'd have guessed that every time he drew on her breast a taut line of fire would run down to her belly and lower, till she felt the empty ache inside?

Who'd have known she'd be so wanton as to rub herself needily against his hand? To delight in the sensation of his long fingers arrowing to her most private core?

Heat fired her cheeks at what she'd done, what she still wanted to do.

It was as if some alien woman had taken over her body. Some daring sensualist she'd never known, who acted on instincts Tamsin hadn't been aware of.

Was it remotely possible this was the real Tamsin, freed of the restraints that had ruled her life so long?

Or was this the result of a life without love or physical demonstrativeness? There'd been few cuddles growing up and no teenage kisses. With Patrick she hadn't ventured far into passion. Perhaps Alaric's caresses had unleashed a pent up longing for physical affection.

She released a shuddering breath. She'd determined to make a new start tonight, be a new woman, free of the crutches she'd used to distance herself from others. But she hadn't meant to go this far!

She hadn't thought…that was the problem.

Tamsin eyed Alaric's powerful frame, lit by a scintillating flash of red. She hadn't thought at all after he'd admitted to being jealous, to wanting her.

Had that been real? Or had it been an excuse to keep his distance because he genuinely hadn't wanted to be with her during the ball? The old Tamsin would have accepted the latter without a second's hesitation. Now she didn't know.

And this hot, heavy seduction scene? Could he have engineered it to provoke the kind of speculation he wanted? To create the illusion they were in a relationship?

But why go so far?

Yet if his desire had been genuine, and it had felt magnificently real when he'd ground himself against her, why the cold shoulder now? He'd reacted violently when she'd tried to touch him and his voice just now had been harsh.

Her lips twisted. If only she had more experience with men, with sex, she might understand!

Had he gone so far simply because she was so obviously, pantingly eager? For Alaric, was one warm female body in the dark as good as another?

The notion sickened her.

It was unfair to think it of him. Yet she remembered that first kiss and how he'd pulled up short when he'd knocked her glasses *and remembered who he was kissing.*

Tamsin bit her lip. All she knew was she wanted him to hold her and take her back to the place she'd been before he'd pulled away. She wanted him to smile and make her feel better.

Listen to her! She was a grown woman, not a child.

A knock sounded on the door and Tamsin started. Yet Alaric turned smoothly as if he'd expected it. Had this been a set-up?

He sent her a long, assessing look and her cheeks burned. Hurriedly she lifted her hands to secure her hair as best she could, then shook out her long skirts. But for the life of her she couldn't move away from the wall at her back. Her knees trembled too much.

'Enter.' Neither his voice nor his appearance gave any hint of what they'd been doing minutes before. *She'd* been the one half naked and wanting. Suddenly the fact that he'd remained fully clothed seemed suspiciously important.

Her throat closed on a knot of distress as she met his unblinking stare.

A steward entered and bowed deeply, his expression wooden. 'Your Highness. Madam.' He cleared his throat. 'I'm sorry to disturb—'

'It's all right.' Alaric's tone was clipped. 'Go on.'

Again the servant bowed. 'The guests are assembled on the terrace, Highness. The fireworks will end in five minutes.'

Alaric nodded, the picture of regal composure. 'Good. I'll be just in time for the toasts.' He turned to her and for a searing moment his gaze held hers, making her heart catapult against her ribs.

'Please accompany Dr Connors to her suite. She was overcome by the exertions of the ball. She doesn't know her way back from this part of the castle.'

The man nodded, his face betraying no emotion. Ridiculously that made Tamsin feel worse. Did Alaric make a habit of seducing women in antechambers? Given his reputation she supposed his servants were used to dealing with his cast off lovers.

A dreadful giggle rose in her throat. The joke was on them because she didn't fit the bill. She hadn't quite made it to the exalted ranks of ex-lover.

Now she probably never would.

'Dr Connors.' Alaric's bow was formal. He straightened and paused, as if waiting for her to speak.

'Your Highness.' A curtsey was beyond her. It was all she could do to stay upright, knees locked.

With a curt nod of acknowledgement he strode out the door, his bearing as rigid as a soldier on parade.

The fantasy was over.

It was time for Cinderella to leave.

At the knock on the door to his suite Alaric paused in the act of shrugging off his jacket.

Could it be her? Had she come to finish what they'd begun? His pulse rocketed, his body tensing in anticipation.

He'd been torn between visiting her now, tonight, and listening to the voice of responsibility that warned she'd been out of her depth. He'd taken advantage. He'd been so intent on seducing her he'd dismissed the need for discretion to protect her or to allow her time to think.

Yet he'd only come here to change from his uniform. He couldn't keep away after that taste of her sweet body.

Now she'd saved him the trouble!

'Come.'

It was an unpleasant shock to see his security chief enter instead. Disappointment surfaced and a disturbing premonition of bad news. The hair rose at his nape as he took in that sombre expression.

'I'm sorry to interrupt, sir, but you gave instructions about Dr Connors' phone calls. You need to hear this.'

The jacket fell from Alaric's hand to a nearby chair and he flexed his fingers. *He didn't want to hear this.*

The report on Tamsin had drawn a blank. The woman was so squeaky clean it was unbelievable. Recently Alaric had set aside his suspicion she might be connected with those trying to disrupt the government. He couldn't believe it.

After tonight he didn't *want* to believe it. He could still taste her cherry sweetness, smell the rich scent of her arousal.

He wanted to turn his back on whatever unpalatable truth awaited. But there was too much at stake.

He couldn't afford to trust his instincts when this was about far more than himself. What of the allegiance he owed Raul? If the document she'd found was genuine at the very least its public release had to be carefully managed. He couldn't fail in this as well.

'When was this call recorded?' He scrubbed a hand over his face, wearier than he'd been in months.

'Before the ball, sir. It was a while before I became aware of the contents. By then the festivities were under way and there was no time to inform you.'

'Very well.' Alaric gestured to a table, curiously unwilling to take the recording in his own hand. 'Leave it.'

His advisor looked as if he'd protest.

Between them hung the knowledge that a stable monarchy was at the core of the nation's wellbeing.

'You can go,' he ordered.

There was only a fractional hesitation. 'Yes, sir.'

The door closed and Alaric was alone. He exhaled slowly, reminding himself of his responsibilities.

Yet the imprint of Tamsin's body branded him. He could almost feel her breasts crushed against him, her hands clutching his hair as he demanded and she reciprocated with a fervour that blasted his control to smithereens. Her scent was on his clothes, his hands. His body was taut with unsated need.

No wonder it felt like betrayal when he took the CD and inserted it into the player.

Long after the recording had ended he stood, staring out into the stark blackness of the night.

Tamsin and Patrick. He knew of the other man from the investigative dossier, though it had been unclear how intimate the pair had been. Now he knew.

They'd been lovers.

His gut roiled queasily at the thought of Tamsin in the arms of another man. In his bed. Alaric's jaw ached as he ground his teeth, trying to harness the overpowering need to do something rash, something violent. It was as well the other man was out of Alaric's way, safe in England.

The way he'd spoken to her in that call! He'd dumped her then expected her to welcome him back with open arms. Alaric registered a tiny flicker of satisfaction that she'd sent him packing. She'd adopted her most glacial schoolmistress voice to get rid of him.

And still Alaric couldn't obliterate the image of her naked in a stranger's arms.

So much for his fancy that her guileless yet fervent kisses were evidence of inexperience. He shook his head. He'd fallen for that buttoned up look, been swayed into believing her prickly reserve and her cover-up clothes meant she was an innocent.

Which showed how she'd impaired his thinking!

The woman was all combustible heat, a born seductress. She'd almost blown the back off his head, just with her cries of encouragement as he'd fondled her.

Alaric planted his palms on the window sill, anchoring himself to the solid rock of the old castle. Belatedly he forced himself to confront the other implication of what he'd heard. He'd deliberately shied from it.

The document she'd found appeared authentic. The date testing proved its age.

He would be the next king of Maritz.

Pain scored his fist as he pounded the sill. His gut hollowed. It was unthinkable! The nation deserved better than him.

Bile rose in his throat and he bowed his head, knowing if he let it, the pain would engulf him. Yet even then he wouldn't be free. He was destined to be alive, whole, unscathed. The ultimate punishment for his failure.

The metallic scent of blood from his grazed fist caught his attention, forcing him to focus. His breathing thickened as he imagined breaking the news to Raul.

Damn! His cousin should be monarch, not him.

Already he was his brother's usurper. How could he oust his cousin, too?

But they had no choice. They'd both been raised to shoulder their responsibilities and face even the most unpalatable duty.

Now, tonight, he had to make arrangements. Raul had to be updated and a second date test of the document organised. He'd have to call on more experts to help prove or disprove the chronicle. The royal genealogist had cautiously advised he couldn't rule out the claim to the throne. But that wasn't good enough. They had to be *certain*.

Yet Alaric had a hollow, sinking feeling each test would only prove his succession.

Fortunately the document was under lock and key. But there was still a danger news would get out before he'd found a way to manage the transition to monarch.

His mind conjured an image of Tamsin and that journo. They'd been so intent they hadn't heard him approach.

Surely she hadn't revealed anything to the newsman. Tamsin had too much integrity. Hadn't she? Doubt sidled through his thoughts and he squashed it furiously.

But finding her with the journo was too coincidental in the circumstances. Even if she was innocent, one unguarded word could shatter the fragile situation. She was so enthusiastic about her work she might inadvertently let something slip. Alaric must ensure that didn't happen.

He shook his head. He couldn't go to her tonight and lose himself in the mindless ecstasy he craved. There were urgent plans to make.

Alaric watched fat snowflakes drift past the window and an idea began to form. The need for Tamsin still gnawed at him, a constant ache. He'd gone beyond the point of no return and abstinence was no longer possible.

He assured himself it was purely physical desire he felt. Anything more…complicated was impossible.

He had to isolate her until arrangements were in place to deal with this mess. That would take time. But wasn't time with Tamsin what he craved?

There was benefit after all in coming from a long line of robber barons and ruthless opportunists.

Kidnapping was virtually an inherited skill.

CHAPTER NINE

'GOOD morning, Tamsin.'

Her shoulders stiffened and heat crawled up her cheeks as that low voice wound its lazy way into her soul.

Her assistant's eyes widened as he looked over her shoulder then darted her a speculative glance. Castle gossip had obviously worked overtime since last night.

Tamsin steadied herself against the archive room's custom built storage units. Finally she turned. She'd been expecting a summons. Even so, facing the man who'd stripped her emotionally bare took all her willpower.

She'd spent the night awake, trying to make sense of the evening's events. For the first few hours she'd half expected Alaric to come to her once his duties were over. Despite her doubts and her pride she'd have welcomed him.

It had only been as dawn arrived she'd realised he had no intention of visiting her. She preferred not to remember her desolation then.

'Hello...' She halted, her mouth drying as that familiar indigo gaze met hers. What should she call him? It had been *Alaric* until his steward had found them together. Then they'd been *Dr Connors* and *Your Highness*. The formality had been a slap in the face, even if it had been an attempt to hide what they'd been doing.

Here he was in her domain, alone, without any secretaries or security staff. *What did he want?*

Her blush burned fiery and she saw something flicker in his eyes. Awareness? Desire? Or distaste?

Tamsin had no idea what he felt. Last night his urgency, his arousal and his words had convinced her he felt the same compulsion she did. But later doubts had crept in.

'How are you today?' His voice held only polite enquiry but she could have sworn she saw something more profound in his expression.

Or was that wishful thinking?

'Well, thank you.' Again she hesitated. Despite his slightly drawn look, she wasn't going to ask him how he was. 'Have you come to see our progress?'

Grimacing at her falsely bright tone, ignoring her staccato pulse, she gestured for him to accompany her to her small office space. She'd feel better knowing every word wasn't overheard.

'Partly.' They reached her desk and Alaric spun round, his gaze intense. 'Why? Do you want to tell me something?'

Tamsin opened her mouth then shut it, frowning.

Last night there'd been no opportunity to tell him about the dating of the manuscript. Alone with him in the antechamber all thought of the document had been blasted from her mind by Alaric and the things he made her feel.

Her gaze skittered away as she recalled what they'd done. Even now desire throbbed deep in her belly and at the apex of her thighs. That persistent current of awareness eroded her efforts to appear unaffected.

She should tell him about the test results, yet she hesitated. Tamsin believed him now when he said he didn't want the crown. For whatever reason, the idea was anathema to him. It was a shame. She'd seen him in action these past couple of weeks and he'd make a terrific king. The easy way he related to people, truly listened to them. His sharp mind and ability to get things done. His need to help.

She read his taut stillness as he awaited her response.

Should she confirm his fears when in her own mind she wasn't fully convinced? Despite Patrick's news some things in the document still needed checking.

Tamsin shrugged stiffly and tidied her desk.

'The new staff have been worth their weight in gold. We're making good headway.'

'Excellent.' He paused as if waiting. 'And the chronicle? Anything interesting in your translations?'

'No.' It wasn't lying. She hadn't uncovered any more revelations.

Alaric's silence eventually made her look up. His expression was unreadable but there was a keenness, an intensity in his scrutiny that unnerved her.

'I should have more information for you soon.'

If she didn't uncover anything to justify her niggle of uncertainty by the end of the week, two days away, she'd break the news about the UK tests.

Strange, this sense that in being cautious she protected Alaric. She'd never met anyone so obviously capable, so patently self-sufficient.

Yet she couldn't shake the feeling that beneath it all, in this one thing Alaric was vulnerable.

'Good.' He reached out and fingered the spine of a catalogue.

Tamsin watched the leisurely caress, recalling how he'd stroked *her* last night. The touch of those large hands had been so exquisite she'd thought she'd shatter if he stopped.

She shivered and suddenly she was caught in the darkening brilliance of his eyes. Heat eddied low and spread in lush, drugging waves as she read his expression. The hungry yearning he couldn't hide.

Realisation slammed into her. Her heart soared.

It was real! Not her imagination. He felt it, too.

Tamsin struggled to inhale oxygen as the air thickened. Excitement revved her pulse, making her heart pound and her head swim. She swiped damp palms down her skirt. The heat inside ignited to a flash fire as his gaze followed the movement then rose, slow and deliberate, to her breasts, her mouth. Her nipples beaded and her lips parted eagerly as if he'd touched her.

'I need to see you, in private.'

'But last night…'

'Last night I should never have started something I couldn't finish.' His mouth twisted in a tight smile that echoed the rigid expression he'd worn as he'd left her in the antechamber. 'Do you really think a few stolen minutes hard and fast against a wall would have been enough?'

Alaric's words made her head swim. Or maybe it was the graphic image that exploded inside her brain. Tamsin's mouth dried as she saw his eyes mirror her excitement and frustration.

'And afterwards…' he paused '…I couldn't come to you.' Before she could ask why he spoke again, his voice darkly persuasive, his eyes glittering. 'But I'm here now.'

Murmured voices approached from the main archive room.

'I want you, Tamsin. Now. Away from interruption.' His voice dropped to a deep resonance that brooked no refusal.

Her breathing shallowed as she teetered on the brink. Part of her was shocked by his unvarnished words. But mostly she was thrilled. Abruptly she nodded, the movement jerky.

She wanted this. The intensity of what was between them scared her, but she would not to hide from it.

She'd done with suppressing her emotions and needs. She'd always love her work but it was no longer enough. She'd be a coward to turn her back on the marvellous feelings Alaric evoked. On the chance to live and experience the passion so blatant in his heavy-lidded look.

Tamsin had no illusions. Whatever he wanted from her, whatever he offered, would be fleeting. But it was genuine. If she had no expectations, except for honesty between them, how could she be hurt?

It was the lies that hurt. The soiled feeling of being used for ulterior purposes, as Patrick had used her.

The unabashed heat in Alaric's eyes, his single-minded focus were honest and headily seductive. Tamsin swallowed hard as excitement fizzed. After a life time of celibacy, she was ready to walk on the wild side.

Alaric had made it clear he didn't believe in love. At the time she'd felt sad for him but now she realised it was a bond between them. She didn't trust herself to try what passed for love again and Alaric was immune to it.

What they shared would be simple, straightforward and satisfying.

'Fifteen minutes.' His mouth barely moved as he murmured the instructions so her approaching colleagues couldn't hear. 'In the courtyard. Your warmest clothes.'

With a searing look he spun on his heel and was gone, leaving Tamsin's heart pounding like she'd run a marathon.

Fifteen minutes. It seemed a lifetime.

Alaric stamped his feet against the cold and refrained from glancing at his watch. She'd be here. He'd read her anticipation. This was one time Tamsin wouldn't object to an ultimatum.

His prim and proper Dr Connors was eager for this too.

He paused in the act of drawing on his gloves. Since when had he thought of Tamsin as 'his'? A sixth sense warning feathered his backbone.

Alaric ignored it.

Tamsin wanted him. He wanted Tamsin. Simple.

And the fact that his intentions weren't completely straightforward?

Alaric would go quietly crazy waiting on the interminable processes to confirm the succession. There was nothing he could *do*. A move to transfer power would be premature and potentially dangerous. Yet he itched for action, to work off the tension coiling within.

With Tamsin he could at least satisfy the lust eating him. This could be his last chance to enjoy freedom before the crown settled on his head. He'd make the most of every moment.

If he became king there'd be no more spur of the moment adventures, no dangerous sports. *No escape.* He shied away from that line of thought.

Tamsin wouldn't be hurt. He'd ensure she was well satisfied.

Despite her complex, fascinating personality, she seemed easy to read. He *wanted* to believe in her. Instinct said she was honest. Yet she'd kept from him the news of the chronicle's age, confirmed last night by her ex-lover. His thoughts snagged on the other man and tension rose.

He hadn't missed her prevarication today, the way her gaze had slid away guiltily as he'd given the perfect opportunity to broach the news.

He was determined to solve the riddle that was Tamsin Connors.

Anticipation coiled in his belly. He acted for the country, but this plan promised personal satisfaction.

Alaric drew on his gloves and glanced at the leaden tint just visible on the horizon. The sooner they left the better, or the forecast snowstorm would catch them too soon. He refused to endanger Tamsin.

If he were alone he'd revel in pitting his strength against the elements. Seeking out danger was one of his few pleasures. Action for the thrill of it. For the breathless affirmation of life in a world of bleak uncertainty.

Or perhaps, he realised in a sombre flash of awareness, in the expectation that eventually his luck would run out?

A death wish?

He gazed up at the bright bowl of the sky, vivid against the mountains, and felt the sizzle of expectation in his veins as he waited for Tamsin.

No. Despite the demons that hounded him, today he could truly say that given the chance he'd choose life.

'Your Highness?'

He swung round to see one of his security staff. 'Yes?'

'I have the report you requested several hours ago. It's only cursory. We'll have more in a day or two.'

At last! Information on this tiresome Patrick who'd rung Tamsin. And on the journo who'd hung on her every word.

He caught movement from the corner of his eye.

Tamsin emerged into the courtyard in a padded anorak and thick trousers. Gone was the glamorous woman who'd entranced him last night. Yet in the sharp light of a winter's morning her beauty defied the handicap of her bulky garments. Her face glowed in the crisp air. Unmarred by heavy glasses her clean, classic bone structure drew his appreciative gaze. Her eyes shone and the lush bow of her lips reminded him of last night's heady pleasure.

Even the way she walked, an easy stride that spoke of supple limbs and natural athleticism, fired his blood.

Besides, he'd discovered at the ball he preferred she hide her luscious body from all male eyes except his.

He was rather fond now of her shapeless outfits. He enjoyed picturing the hidden curves beneath. Especially as he had every intention of stripping those garments away for his pleasure very soon.

Alaric couldn't remember any woman getting so deeply under his skin. And he hadn't even slept with her!

'Your Highness?'

He swung back to the man patiently waiting.

'Thank you.' He nodded and took the envelope. No time now to satisfy his curiosity with Tamsin approaching. He stuffed the envelope into a pocket and rezipped his all-weather jacket. 'That's all for now. If anything urgent comes up I have my mobile phone.'

The other man bowed and stepped away as Tamsin reached him. Alaric turned, reminding himself not to touch, not yet, lest his brittle control snap.

Looking down into her bright eyes he realised this felt right. *She felt right.*

He smiled. Not a deliberate ploy to entice her but because for the first time in recent memory genuine happiness flared. He'd almost forgotten how good it felt.

'Where are we going?' They were the first words Tamsin had spoken in twenty minutes.

She'd been tongue-tied by the enormity of her feelings and the potency of what she saw in Alaric's eyes. When he looked at her, his gaze smoky and possessive, tendrils of awareness curled through her, spiralling tighter. Just the graze of his gloved hand on hers as he helped her take her seat had made her breathless.

Once they were under way disbelief, delight and sheer joy had kept her silent as she watched the forest slide past. Never in her wildest dreams had she envisaged a horse-drawn sleigh ride across pristine powder snow! It was a romantic fantasy.

They threaded their way through dense forest, emerging now and then into glades where the brilliant blue sky dazzled as it shone on diamond bright snow.

'We're visiting a small hunting lodge in the mountains. The road is impassable and the only way in is by sleigh.'

It sounded thrillingly intimate.

Alaric turned from guiding the horses and bestowed a single, lingering look. Instantly, despite the chill air, heat blazed through Tamsin. Beneath the layers of heavy blankets he'd tucked around her she was burning up.

'We'll be uninterrupted there.'

'I see.' Was that her voice, husky and low?

One black eyebrow arched and a crease arrowed down his cheek as he smiled. 'I knew you would.' His rich velvet voice held a hum of anticipation that matched hers. 'I've left orders that the lodge is absolutely off limits.'

His grin worked magic, loosening the final constricting ties of doubt. Under that look Tamsin felt buoyantly alive and strong, as if she could do anything. Dare anything.

Why be nervous? They were two adults. They both wanted this. Still her heart thudded against her ribs.

So what if she was a novice? Alaric had enough experience for them both.

Whatever the next few hours held, she wouldn't regret the decision to accompany him. Being with Alaric was like the thrill she'd felt scaling that climbing wall, recognising but defying the dangerous drop below. The glow of pleasure, knowing she'd dared the risk and triumphed, had been worth the initial doubt.

How different to the hemmed in half-life she'd led! How frightening to think that just weeks ago she'd have been too nervous, too wary to take this step.

Alaric turned back to the horses and Tamsin wriggled against the seat, luxuriating in an effervescent tingle of anticipation.

In the knowledge that at the end of the journey they would finish what had begun last night.

The whoosh and slide of the sleigh and the tinkle of harness bells echoing in the pine-scented forest reminded her they were completely alone. There were no staff, no members of the public seeking Alaric's attention. No one to look askance at his choice of companion.

Companion. For a moment the word jangled a discordant note. But even the memory of his original proposition, that she accompany him as a ruse, couldn't dim Tamsin's delight.

This was now. Just the two of them. *This was real.*

The admiration in his eyes made her feel like a princess. She intended to enjoy it while it lasted.

Looking up, Tamsin noticed slate grey clouds encroaching. 'That looks like bad weather coming.'

'It's nothing to worry about.'

It was on the tip of her tongue to protest. Surely those clouds presaged snow. But it was easier to sink back and ignore them. Alaric knew this place. Perhaps she was wrong and the clouds were moving away.

Finally they arrived in a clearing, hemmed in on two sides by the mountain. Below spread more forest and in the distance a vista of Alps and valleys.

'This is your lodge?' She'd expected something tiny. She'd almost allowed herself to forget Alaric was royalty. On the re-membrance a tremor of doubt buzzed through her and she sat straighter.

'It was built by my great-great-great-grandfather Rudi as a retreat. For when he wanted to escape the court.'

She eyed the substantial building: traditional Ruvingian archi-tecture but overgrown and embellished with mullioned windows, a forest of chimneys and even a turret. 'Let me guess. He didn't want to rough it.'

Alaric laughed and delight strummed her nerves. Soon...

'Rudi enjoyed his pleasures.' Alaric's glittering look made her press her thighs close against a needy hollow ache.

'You're cold. Let's get you inside.' Deftly he flicked the reins. Ten minutes later they were in a huge stable.

'You go ahead while I see to the horses.'

'Can't I help?' She'd rather watch Alaric's easy movements as he unhitched the horses.

'No.' His eyes held hers and heat pulsed. 'Go and get warm. Make yourself at home. I won't be long, I promise.'

The lodge was unlocked and she stepped into a flagged hall. Warmth hit her as she stared up at the staircase leading down on two sides. Antlers lined the room and a vivid mural ran around the top of the walls.

Tugging off her cap and gloves she paused in the act of undoing her jacket as she followed the scenes of revellers enjoying the bounty of the forest. There were plenty of buxom maids in attendance.

Her lips turned up wryly. Maybe Alaric's ancestor had been a connoisseur of women, too.

She hung up her jacket, letting her mind skim past the idea of Alaric with other women. She unzipped her boots and left them beside the antique tiled oven that warmed the hall. Someone had prepared the place for their arrival.

'Hello?' Tamsin wandered through sitting rooms, a library, a dining room that seated twenty, a kitchen and storage room, but found no one. Yet there was enough food to feed a small army.

Curious, she walked up the staircase. Its balustrade was carved with animals: hares, deer, hounds, even a boar. The whimsy appealed. Had old Rudi possessed a smile and a laugh as fascinating as his great-great-great-grandson's?

Alaric would be here soon.

Her heart gave a great thump and began to gallop. She moved on till she reached a pair of double doors and hesitated. There was something intimate about investigating the bedrooms. But Alaric had said to make herself at home.

Turning the handle she entered. Her breath caught as she turned to take it in.

The turret room.

It was round, windows set into curved, cream walls. Velvet curtains of azure blue were pulled aside, allowing sunlight to pour across thickly cushioned window seats and a gorgeous old Turkish rug in a kaleidoscope of colours. A fireplace was set ready for the match and opposite it was the biggest four poster bed she'd seen in her life. Drapes of blue velvet were tied back to beautifully turned posts and the headboard was carved with the arms of the Ruvingian royal house.

The reminder of Alaric's status stopped her, a splinter of harsh reality in her pleasant daydream.

Prince and commoner. It was too far-fetched. Too unreal.

'I hoped I'd find you here.'

Tamsin spun round as Alaric closed the door. Its click made her jump.

'I couldn't find anyone.' Her voice emerged too high. She watched his long silent stride. Something inside her shivered and her pulse danced.

'We're the only ones here.' His lips curved up but his eyes were darkly intent.

'I see.'

She wanted this, so why had her tongue stuck to the roof of her mouth? Why did she feel suddenly nervous?

'So you want to talk now?'

He raised an eyebrow. 'Talk? What about?'

'When you came to the archives you said you wanted…'

Slowly he shook his head as he paced closer. 'I didn't mention conversation.' He stopped so near she smelled warm flesh and horse and citrus soap. She breathed deep and put out a steadying hand to the post behind her.

She was quaking but not, she registered, in fear.

'You knew that.' His gaze snared hers and her stomach dipped. 'Didn't you, Tamsin?'

She nodded. No point prevaricating. She knew exactly what he'd wanted. Why he'd invited her here.

'Would *you* like to talk?' He gestured to a couple of chairs she hadn't noticed to one side of the room.

'No.' The single syllable was all she could manage.

'What do you want, Tamsin?' He purred her name and the final thread of resistance unravelled inside her.

She lifted her face to look him in the eye. What she saw there gave her the courage to be honest.

'I want to make love with you. Now.'

CHAPTER TEN

HER words blasted away Alaric's barely formed suspicion that she was nervous.

It wasn't nerves that made her eyes widen as he crossed the room. It was excitement. Despite her initial hesitation when he kissed her, and her occasional air of other-worldliness, Tamsin was no shrinking virgin. Last night's phone call from her ex-lover had made that clear.

Alaric breathed deep as anticipation roared through him. This was exactly what he needed. A mutually satisfying interlude with a woman who knew how to give and take pleasure generously. Tamsin's passion last night left him in no doubt this would be an erotically fulfilling encounter.

He shoved to the back of his mind the knowledge that he was taking advantage. That his motives bringing her here were complex and he was keeping things from her.

But he couldn't feel guilt. Not when he looked at Tamsin and knew only one thing drove him now: the purely personal need to claim her. Make her his.

'It will be my absolute pleasure to make love to you,' he murmured, his gaze trawling her tense form and coming to rest on her parted lips.

He'd waited so long for this. Too long.

He palmed her soft cheek, noting with delight the way she tilted her head up, instinctively seeking his mouth.

But he'd learned his lesson. Kissing Tamsin would unleash a desire so combustible he'd lose control in moments. This time he'd hold back to savour every exquisite detail for as long as possible. He had no illusions that the first time would be over almost before it began.

Just as well they had leisure for a second time and a third. And more. Tamsin would be here, his, for as long as he needed her.

'Let your hair down.'

She blinked at the rough growl edging his voice but lifted her hands. Rippling swathes of dark glossy hair cascaded around her shoulders. In the bright wintry light auburn tints gleamed. So rich. So unexpected. Just like Tamsin.

He took a slippery fistful. The scent of sweet summer meadows. Skeins soft as satin slid against his lips.

He was hungry for the taste of her. Hard with wanting.

'Now your pullover.' He wanted to strip her himself but he didn't trust himself to retain control.

Next time.

No, she wouldn't have a chance to get dressed before he had her again. His groin hardened as blood pumped faster.

For an instant Tamsin hesitated then she hauled the wool over her head. As she stretched her arms high a sliver of pale skin appeared at her waist. In an instant his hands were there, slipping beneath her grey shirt.

She stilled, half out of her pullover, as he slid fingers across warm flesh that trembled under his touch.

So deliciously sensitive. Her delicate little shudder of pleasure delighted him as his hands skimmed her waist and dipped below the waistband of her trousers to explore the curve of her hips.

By the time she'd discarded the pullover he'd tunnelled beneath her shirt, up, up, till all she had to do was lift her arms again and it was gone, too.

Alaric tossed it over his shoulder as he feasted on the sight of her. Her peaches and cream complexion was flushed to a soft rose pink. He'd never known a woman to blush all over. The novelty of it tugged at something deep inside and he felt an unexpected moment of protectiveness.

His breath sawed in his throat as he traced the tell tale colour from her cheeks, past her lips, down to the base of her throat where her pulse pattered hard and fast. He stroked lower, down the upper slope of her breasts.

Her nipples puckered in welcome beneath her ivory bra. Functional, with a minimum of lacy edging and a tiny bow between her breasts, on Tamsin the plain bra looked sexier than the most revealing demi-cup or lace-up corset.

Alaric's breath grew hoarse and heavy as he slipped his hands to her breasts. Warm, perfect, full, they filled his palms as she pressed forward, her eyelids flickering closed.

Fire exploded in his belly as he held her soft bounty in his hands. Gently he caressed and her head lolled back, her neck arched invitingly.

His mouth was a hair's breadth from her scented throat when he recalled his scattered wits. No kisses. Not yet.

He dragged himself back, wincing at the shaft of discomfort in his groin.

Alaric dealt with the snap on her trousers and the zip easily, pushing the fabric down, down those long, lithe legs till at his urging she stepped out of them. Even the act of stripping her long grey and black striped socks was a sensual indulgence as he crouched before her. The intimate heat of her sex was so close. The silkiness of her calves teased as he skimmed the socks down. The seductive arch of each foot distracted as he tugged the socks free.

Low before her he was tempted to lean in and explore her feminine secrets with his lips and tongue. But he was too close to the edge to risk it.

Instead he allowed his fingertips to skim her knees and thighs as he rose, lingering for a moment at her knickers, where her heat beckoned, over her belly, breasts and up to cup her jaw.

She was sensational. All soft curves, taut lines and delicate angles. Pure female seduction. Just looking at her almost tipped him over the edge.

Eyes bright as gold stared up into his, dazzling him. The impact of her sunburst gaze thumped through his chest and showered sparks through every nerve and muscle.

'You're wearing too many clothes.' Tamsin's voice was hoarse, almost unrecognisable. He felt a kick of satisfaction low in his gut that she was as desperate as he.

'Easily remedied.' With a violent movement he dragged his shirt and sweater up and off, flinging them behind him.

Though warm, the air was cool to his burning skin. Soft palms landed on his chest, fingers splaying. Tamsin explored his pectorals, scraping her nails tantalisingly over his hard nipples, trailing her hands to his belly.

In a flash his trousers were open and he shoved them down, balancing on one leg then another as he discarded underwear, socks and trousers in record time.

Belatedly he recalled the condom in his back pocket and stooped to retrieve it. There was a box of them in the bedside table but watching Tamsin's face as she took in his naked body, he knew those few metres to the table might as well be a hundred kilometres.

Tearing the wrapper with his teeth, he deftly rolled on the protection, pleasure spiking at Tamsin's expression of shocked excitement. The way she stared he could have been a demi-god, a hero, not an earthbound man with feet of clay. His blood beat hard and fast as his hands dropped away.

He stepped forward.

Alaric loomed closer and Tamsin backed up.

She hadn't intended to. It was instinctive, an unplanned bid to escape a man who suddenly seemed dangerous in a primitive, ultra-physical way she'd never known.

The reality of Alaric the man, of what they were doing, hit her full force.

He was so big, so heavily aroused; a sliver of anxiety pierced the fog of desire. He could bend her to his will and she wouldn't be able to resist. Whatever he demanded of her he could take.

An age old female wariness sped down her backbone. It had nothing to do with his royal rank and everything to do with Alaric as a virile, dominant male.

The cool slap of the high footboard against the back of her legs brought her up short. As did his puzzled expression.

'Tamsin?' He stood where he was, only reached out one arm to her. Like the rest of him it was powerfully corded with muscle. Yet as she looked she saw his fingers tremble.

She gulped down the panic that had bubbled out of nowhere and looked into his eyes, glazed with hot desire yet questioning. This time her brain kicked into gear.

When she'd watched him roll on the condom, his eyes had eaten her up with a fierceness that thrilled and terrified her. When he'd approached she'd let fear of the unknown swamp the surge of desire.

Now she saw that despite Alaric's raw hunger, he was the same man she'd come to know these last weeks. A man who'd been honest and straight with her. Who desired her.

A man she could trust.

Maybe every woman felt that tinge of fear the first time, confronted with such unvarnished lust and the stunning reality of naked male arousal.

Her lips curved up in a wobbly smile as she realised very few women were gifted with a first lover as gorgeous as Alaric. Just looking at him made her heart throb so fast she could scarcely catch her breath.

This was what she wanted. She refused to walk away from something that felt so good, so right.

She just needed courage.

Eyes holding his, Tamsin reached around and fumbled her bra undone, letting it fall with a shake of her arms.

Alaric drew a huge breath, his chest expanding mightily. His outstretched hand curled and fell away.

Her unbound breasts felt impossibly full, the nipples hardening to aching points as his heated gaze dropped. Fire scorched a trail across her breasts and lower.

Following the direction of his gaze, Tamsin hooked her thumbs in the sides of her panties. There she hesitated as her inbuilt urge to cover herself fought the need to offer herself to Alaric. A lifetime's habit was strong, but far stronger was the magic she felt when he looked at her with such longing.

She felt desirable. Desired. Feminine. Powerful. Needy.

Without giving herself time to think she shoved her underwear down, felt the slide of fine cotton against her legs and the waft of air against her skin. All over.

'You have no idea how badly I want you.' Alaric's voice was a rough blur of words that tugged at something low in her belly. Pleasure coursed through her as his eyes sparked blue fire.

A second later he lifted her up and onto the mattress.

His hands were so large they almost spanned her waist. His sure grip reinforced the physical differences between them. Yet this time her vulnerability didn't bring fear. A delicious flutter of excitement filled her.

With one fluid, powerful movement he pushed her up the bed and sank down on her. Senses on overload, she gasped for breath, but nothing could calm the spiralling excitement that drove her on. She was hemmed in, surrounded by him and nothing had ever felt so perfect.

Arms closing round his torso, Tamsin pressed her mouth to Alaric's neck, his shoulder, tasting the spicy salt flavour of him. Sinking into the mattress, soft velvet caressed her back while her breasts, belly and legs rubbed against satiny skin, powerfully bunched muscles and coarse hair that teased every nerve ending.

He was so…male. So intriguing.

So sexy.

He moved and she swallowed a gasp of pleasure at the sensation of his broad chest sliding against her breasts. Delight was a rippling wave engulfing her, surging again with each tiny move, each touch.

Driven by instinct, she'd invited this. Yet she'd been unprepared for the stunning reality of Alaric's body against hers. Theoretical knowledge only took a girl so far.

Alaric slid a fraction and his erection pressed against her belly. Instantly the hollow ache inside intensified and her hips strained up against him.

Thankfully her body knew what it was doing. Instinct would make up for her lack of practical knowledge.

Then Alaric's mouth captured her nipple and Tamsin lost the capacity for thought as wet heat tugged at her, drawing blood-hot wires of tension through her arching body.

She needed…she needed…

'I love it that you're so hot and ready for me.' His hoarse voice was the most thrilling thing Tamsin had ever heard and the possessive splay of his hand across her feminine mound would have brought her up off the bed if she hadn't been anchored by his strong frame.

She wriggled her hips and he moved, nudging her legs apart with one solid thigh. Eagerly she complied.

'Yes. Like that,' he growled, raising his head and spearing her with a searing look of approval.

Vaguely she noticed the way Alaric's skin stretched taut over that magnificent bone structure, his mouth a grim line of tension.

His hand moved, arrowing unerringly through damp curls and folds that felt plump and hyper-sensitive. Tamsin's body jolted as long fingers slid down.

She couldn't gasp enough breath. Her chest pounded and she stretched her arms up to grab his shoulders, digging into taut, hot flesh. He said something she couldn't hear over the roaring in her ears as he looked to where his fingers stroked again, further, faster.

Tamsin bit her lip against the sob of pleasure rising in her throat. But she couldn't stop the way her body moved into his caress. Confidently, needily.

When he met her gaze again there was a feral glitter in his eyes. He looked like a marauder, a ruthless barbarian intent on plunder. As if she were the bounty he intended to take for himself.

She loved it!

Slipping her hands along those wide shoulders, she clamped her fingers behind his head, desperately burrowing through his thick hair for a good grip. Pulling down, she raised herself and plastered a raw, breathless, open-mouthed kiss on his lips.

For one fragile moment he seemed suspended above her, unmoving. Then he sank onto her again and passion erupted.

Their kiss was fervent, impatient, and his caress between her legs changed. No longer Alaric's hand but something longer, throbbing with a will of its own as he clamped his hands beneath her buttocks and tilted her hips.

'I'm sorry. I can't hold off any longer.'

Tamsin barely processed his words when he shifted and she felt heat nudge the entrance between her legs. Fire flooded her womb at the spiralling whorls of anticipation created by that blunt touch. At last!

His lips closed on hers again, inviting her to join him in pleasure as his tongue pushed greedily into her mouth. At the same time his hold on her bottom tightened and his hips plunged against hers.

One long, slow thrust stretched her body till she was taut, impaled and impossibly full. Gone was the heady passion, replaced in that instant by the first flutterings of panic. Every muscle stiffened and her eyes snapped open.

Startled ink blue irises stared back. Alaric lifted his mouth from hers and sucked in a shaky breath as he pulled away.

Surprisingly, the sensation of his withdrawal instantly distressed her and she clamped her knees against his hips. She didn't want him gone! She just didn't want the scary feeling that he was too big for her. That despite their desire, this wasn't going to work.

'Alaric?' Tamsin didn't care that the word wobbled or that he could hear the entreaty in her voice. Pride had no place here. 'Please.' She didn't know what she expected him to do. She only knew she couldn't bear it to end like this.

A gusty sigh riffled her hair and his head dropped between his bunched shoulders. Tendons stood out on his neck and arms and inside she felt a pulse where the tip of his erection moved.

Response shivered through her at that tiny, impossibly erotic movement. Involuntarily she twitched, circling her hips and his breath stopped.

In answer he withdrew a fraction then slowly pushed forward. This time it didn't feel quite so scary. Or maybe that was his warm breath blowing on her nipple, teasing the aroused bud and distracting her from the slide of his body away then back again.

The next time he eased forward her hips lifted to meet him and he sank a fraction further. But before she had time to register the sensations he was gone again, pulling away and leaving her frustratingly empty.

The fourth time he began to move she anticipated him, arching upwards simultaneously, then gasping as a fiery spark of pleasure flared at the point of friction. Her breath hitched and instantly he stilled, his breathing harsh and uneven.

Tamsin waited but he didn't move. What now? Had he decided this wasn't going to work? Her hands fisted at his shoulders and she bit her lip against the protest that hovered on her tongue.

Then she saw the pulse at the base of Alaric's neck, thudding out of control. He was waiting for her. Trying to accommodate her fear, her discomfort. The rigidity of his body, the way his broad chest heaved like overworked bellows told their own story of the toll this took.

Suddenly this wasn't just about her. Tamsin felt ashamed by her self-absorption.

Tentatively she slipped her hands down his body, feeling muscles flinch at her light caress. Daringly she reached out and smoothed her palms over his hips, down to his taut, rounded buttocks that felt so good under her increasingly needy touch. She wanted to explore him all over, she realised with a shock.

A spasm shook him as she tightened her hold and pulled him towards her. For an instant he resisted then allowed himself to be tugged closer, inside. Even further than before. This time instead of panic, Tamsin felt a niggle of a strange new sensation. A gnawing need for more. When he withdrew she followed. When she urged him close he slid even deeper and a shaky sigh of pleasure escaped her lips.

Gradually, a fraction at a time, their movements became rhythmic and fluid. Tamsin hated each withdrawal and welcomed each thrust, even when it seemed he plunged impossibly deep. Yet even that felt right. More than right. Fantastic.

Now she revelled in the way he drove so far within her.

Alaric's head lifted and his gaze locked with hers. It felt absurdly as if he touched a part of her no medical scan would ever identify. As if he caressed her very soul with his eyes, his body, his tenderness.

Tamsin's breath sucked out at the heat glazing Alaric's eyes and the reflection there of her own overwhelming need.

Lightning flickered as electricity jolted through her body. His tempo increased, her body tightened, achingly close to some unseen goal. A shudder raked him, raked her, and their rhythm rocked out of control into a fierce pounding beat that brought the world tumbling around them.

A gasping scream rent the air as Tamsin fell into pleasure. Everything swam around her except dark blue eyes, fixed on hers in the maelstrom of exquisite delight. Then, with a hoarse shout, Alaric followed her and she drew him close with trembling arms and an overflowing heart.

CHAPTER ELEVEN

A VIRGIN.

Alaric shook his head as if to dislodge the knowledge that weighted him. How had he convinced himself Tamsin was experienced?

He doused his head under the basin's cold tap but that didn't obliterate the voice of his conscience. He'd seduced a virgin. Deliberately set her up to fall into his bed.

He grimaced. He'd shown little consideration for her inexperience as he'd hammered her untried body.

It was no excuse that the feel of her virginal body tight around him had been the ultimate aphrodisiac.

Experienced as he was he had no defence against the pleasure she offered so unstintingly.

Would he have held back if he'd suspected the truth?

Nothing on earth would have held him back. He was as bad as that old roué Rudi, the ancestor who'd designed the place to keep his scandalous liaisons from prying eyes. Alaric's shoulders tightened. No, he was worse. The women Rudi had bedded had reputedly been experienced. Even his father had kept that rule.

Hell! This was a new take on *noblesse oblige.*

Alaric raised his eyes to the bathroom mirror, expecting, as ever, to see his sins marked on his face. But as usual he was the same. Unblemished. Outwardly whole. As if the darkness within were a figment of his imagination.

What right had *he*, of all men, to take her innocence? She deserved a man who could give her more.

Familiar pain lanced his chest, a physical manifestation of his guilt. The ghosts stirred and he waited for the inevitable chill to engulf him.

Yet there was only the remembered heat of Tamsin's sweet body. The warmth of her eyes, looking up as if he'd done something heroic rather than ravish her virginity. And around his heart was an unfamiliar glow.

Alaric shook his head again, splattering the mirror and his shoulders with icy droplets. This was no time for flights of fancy. He grabbed a towel and roughly dried his hair. With a final accusing glare at the mirror he left.

'You were gone a long time.'

He stopped mid-stride. He'd thought Tamsin would be asleep. Or was that his conscience hoping she'd be too exhausted to confront him?

His skin tightened as he looked up to find her propped against pillows, her hair a sensuous tangle of silk on pale shoulders. A flush coloured her cheeks and her lips were plump and enticing after those bruising kisses.

Alaric's belly went into freefall. His penis throbbed into life and he wished he'd thought to take his clothes with him into the bathroom.

Colour intensified in her cheeks as her gaze skated down. His arousal grew, as if eager for her attention.

'You're...ready again?' Her voice faltered and he winced, imagining her nerves.

'Don't worry.' He paced to the foot of the bed where his clothes lay scattered. 'I'm not going to pounce on you.'

'You're not?' He imagined a thread of disappointment in her tone and gritted his teeth. He looked for any excuse to have her again, even pretending she was eager for more.

'Of course not. You're a virgin and—'

'Was.' The flush intensified, spreading over her throat and down to where she clamped a snowy sheet against her breasts. Alaric's gaze lingered on the way they rose and fell. 'What's that got to do with anything?'

'Sorry?' He'd lost the thread of the conversation.

'The fact that I was a virgin. What's that got to do with not having sex again?'

He liked the way she said 'having sex' with a slight hesitancy. It reminded him of her innocently incendiary kisses and the initially faltering yet devastating way she'd taken him into her body.

He scooped up some clothing. Damn. It was her shirt. Where was his?

'Didn't you like it?' Now she sounded frosty. Good. They could do with reducing the temperature around here.

He grabbed something else off the floor. Her trousers, still warm from her body. Another reminder of the speed of their coupling. He should be ashamed. It was sheer luck she'd climaxed. Once he'd buried himself fully he'd been incapable of holding back to ensure her pleasure.

'Alaric? You didn't like it?'

He gritted his teeth. Thinking about what they'd done spun him to the edge of control. 'Men don't perform when they're not enjoying themselves.'

'Then why not again?'

He didn't meet her eyes. Coward that he was he turned to scan the room for his trousers.

'Wasn't once enough?' Surely his unskilled efforts didn't merit a repeat. 'Besides, you'll be sore. You're not used to sex.' The words were brutal but it was all he could do to keep talking when he wanted to vault into that bed, tug her close and take her again. The battle against his selfish, baser self was all consuming.

'I'm not sore.'

'You will be.'

'So you're an expert on virgins?'

'Of course not! I'm no expert on innocence.' He spun round, his temper flaring under the goad of her lashing words. *Do you really think I'd have brought you here if I'd known the truth about you? This wouldn't have happened!'*

A half-smile stiffened on her lips and the bright flare of gold in her eyes dimmed. Too late he realised she'd been teasing, inadvertently zeroing in on his guilty conscience.

He raked a hand through his hair and breathed deep. His brain wasn't working and the words shooting from his mouth were all wrong. He couldn't think straight. Not with her sitting there all demure invitation, tempting him.

He'd thought to kill two birds with one stone. Keep Tamsin where she couldn't spill any headline news and sate his hunger. Suddenly, though, this had become something else altogether. The stakes, and his own culpability, had grown enormously.

There was a flurry of movement as she clambered out of bed, dragging a coverlet. Her chin was set belligerently but he couldn't read her face. She kept her expressive eyes downcast as she walked the length of the bed.

Automatically he backed away, knowing if she got too close he'd do something reprehensible, like grab her and plant kisses all over her petal soft skin.

At his movement she stopped so abruptly she seemed to shudder to a halt. Close up her mouth looked pinched tight, her face drawn.

He wanted to ease her hurt, tease her into smiling, but his light-hearted seduction skills had deserted him the moment he'd taken her in his arms.

His hands fisted as he watched her bend to retrieve some clothing. It was only as she rose that he caught the glitter of moisture at the corners of her averted eyes.

'Tamsin?' He stepped near and she stiffened. Pain scraped his heart. 'Don't cry. Please.'

'Don't be absurd. I'm not crying.' She sniffed and turned away, the bedclothes twisting around her. 'You've made it clear this afternoon was a monumental disappointment. If you don't mind I'd like to get dressed. Alone. I'll return to the castle as soon as possible.'

She shuffled away, hampered by the long trail of material which slid down to reveal the voluptuous curve of her spine.

'You've got it wrong!' He closed the space between them till he could smell the scent of her skin and the sunshine in her hair. Close enough to see her bare flesh prickle with cold. Or distress.

'Don't!' She breathed deep, her back to him. 'Please don't. I understand. I may be naïve but I'm not dumb. You wanted it to look like we were having an affair. To fool those other women. So you brought me here and…' Her averted head dropped low, revealing the vulnerable arch of her nape.

'I misunderstood.' Her voice was a whisper now and he had to crane to hear. 'I thought…you know what I thought. And when you said you didn't want to talk…'

Her head jerked up and around and she pinioned him with a furious amber stare.

'No! It's your fault as much as mine. You *know* what you implied. You let me think…' She bit her lip and swallowed hard. 'You didn't say anything *then* about only wanting experienced women!'

'Because it's not true.'

'So it's just me.' She blinked and turned away. 'I see. Well, I'm sorry I don't come up to your *royal* standards.' The wobble in her voice gouged a hole through his chest.

'I didn't mean that.' He planted a hand on her shoulder but she shrugged it off and moved to the head of the bed. 'Tamsin! You don't understand.'

'Leave me alone, Alaric. I was stupid ever to imagine you'd be attracted to a woman like me. I got carried away with the fairy tale, that's all. It must happen to you all the time. Women with stars in their eyes.'

She dropped her clothes on the bed in front of her and bent to step into her panties but the coverlet got in the way. With an exclamation of impatience she thrust it aside, letting it slide to the floor.

Frustration filled him. Self-contempt and annoyance at finding himself on the defensive. Plus a sexual hunger even greater than before. *One taste hadn't been enough.*

He reached for her again.

'Does it *feel* like I'm not attracted?' With his hands on her hips he jerked her back so his arousal pressed blatantly against her buttocks. He almost groaned at how right that felt.

The breath hissed from her lungs as he slid his palms over her belly and ground his hips in a slow rotation that left him light-headed.

'I want you, Tamsin. I brought you here with the express intention of getting you into my bed.' He slipped one hand down to the moist heat between her thighs and felt her shudder as he homed in on that most sensitive of spots.

'Or not. Anywhere would do. The sleigh, the barn, the kitchen. I don't care. But I've been trying, unsuccessfully, to keep my distance because I realised too late how I've taken advantage. I'm responsible—'

'You're not responsible for me.' Her defiance was belied by her throaty pleasure as her lower body moved a fraction against his stroking fingers. Her responsiveness cracked his resolve further and he slid himself provocatively against her cushioning curves.

'I'm responsible for taking your innocence.'

'You're talking antiquated rubbish. It's my business when I choose to lose my virginity.'

'That doesn't diminish my culpability.'

'Oh!' With a violent jerk Tamsin freed herself and swung to face him. Before he could prevent her she snatched up the coverlet and hid all that firm, glorious flesh. 'You're infuriating! Do you always take the world on your shoulders?'

Alaric watched passion animate her features and felt desire cloud his brain. 'I knew what I was doing. You didn't.'

She rolled her eyes. 'You know, women even have the vote these days. We're capable of making decisions about who we want to make love to.'

Make love. It hit him with a jolt that for the first time the euphemism seemed more apt than 'having sex'.

Ridiculous. What they'd shared was carnal pleasure at its most raw. Pleasure so complete he could no longer resist its pull. Love didn't enter into it.

'All right. Who do you want to make love to?' Alaric loomed towards her. *His conscience could go hang.*

Tamsin shuffled back, eyes widening as she realised she was trapped against the bed.

'I want to go back to the castle.'

'No, you don't. You want to climb on that mattress and let me show you the things we didn't have time for earlier.' Heat sizzled under his skin just watching her shocked delight as she processed his words. The furtive way her eyes darted to the bed. 'I want it too.'

She tilted her chin defiantly and her grip tightened on the bedspread. 'It didn't sound like it a minute ago. Are you sure?'

'Totally.'

'Why?'

Why? The question flummoxed him. Couldn't she feel the erotic charge leaping between them? Didn't she understand what they'd shared had been remarkable, despite its brevity? So wondrous, so perfect no one in their right mind could walk away from it. He speared a hand through his hair in frustration. *Why did women always want to talk?*

The belligerent jut of her finely honed jaw said she wasn't going to make this easy.

'Because I've wanted you so long,' he murmured, finally giving himself up to the truth. 'Since I walked into the library and saw your sexy leg swinging above my head. Since I discovered a woman who challenges and intrigues and piques my curiosity. Who's passionate about something as complex as translating ancient books and as simple as a waltz. Who's not overawed by my title. Who's not charmed by wealth and prestige and isn't afraid to tell me what she thinks.'

'This isn't about duping those other women?' She gnawed on her lip and hurt shaded her fine eyes.

Alaric's mouth thinned and he silently cursed the fact he'd used that excuse to keep her close. If he'd known how unsure she was about her own desirability he'd never have done it. It had taken him too long to understand that her professional confidence hid deep vulnerability.

'It's got nothing to do with anyone but us.'

He lifted a hand and stroked the hair from her face, revelling in the way she swayed infinitesimally towards him. 'You're the most naturally sexy woman. Yet you hide your sensuality from everyone but me.' He smiled and slid a hand down her throat to where her pulse thrummed.

'Do you know what a turn on it is, being the only one in on your secret? Seeing your buttoned up shirts and long skirts, your sensible shoes and no-nonsense bun? Knowing that beneath is a siren who makes my pulse race with just one demure glance from those brilliant eyes?'

'I…' She shook her head as if words failed her.

He smoothed his index finger down her brow. 'Even that tiny frown you have when you're concentrating gets me. And the way you pout your lips over a knotty problem.' He breathed deep, trying to slow his escalating heartbeat.

'Every time I visit the archives and find you poring over papers I want to slam the door shut. I want to take you there, against the storage units. Or on that massive desk. You wouldn't believe how often I've imagined it.'

Colour flared in Tamsin's pale face and her mouth softened. Alaric bent his head, letting his breath feather her temple, torturing himself with the scent of her.

'You've imagined it too. I can see it in your face.'

For the first time Tamsin was bereft of speech. She just stood, staring up at him in mute appeal.

Unfamiliar sensations stirred. Something deep inside swelled, filling the tattered remnants of his soul.

'It's all right,' he murmured, wondering if he was reassuring himself as well as her. 'I'll make it all right.' He let his hand drop. 'But only if you want.'

Silence thundered in the air, pulsing like a living thing as their eyes meshed. Something unfamiliar twisted in his chest as he waited for her response. Something more than desire. Something far stronger.

'I want you too, Alaric.'

Relief speared him. She was his. For now.

That's all he wanted. He ignored the half-formed idea that there was more than simple sex between them.

Making love…

No. Emotional connections were too dangerous.

But sex…sex he could handle. Sex they would both enjoy. A final fling before he faced the burdens of the crown. Desperation edged his movements as he wrenched the coverlet from her slack hold. Rosy nipples like proud dusky buds pouted just for him.

He reached out to the bedside table and yanked open the drawer, unerringly finding one of the packets he needed.

'This time,' he promised with a taut smile, 'we're going to take things slow.'

Hours later Tamsin lay, limbs deliciously weighted, so exhausted she felt like she floated on a cloud above the huge four poster bed. The shift and rustle of logs burning in the grate was the only sound. Never had she felt so languid, yet so alert to each sensation. The tickle of hair across her shoulders as she burrowed beneath the covers, the awareness of her body. Especially those parts where Alaric had devoted such lingering attention.

She squeezed her thighs together, conscious of the achy, empty feeling just *there*. Not sore. More *aware*.

Her lips curved dreamily. It wasn't merely what they'd done together. Warmth like honeyed chocolate flowed through her as she remembered Alaric's words.

She wouldn't be human, wouldn't be female if she wasn't thrilled by the thought of him secretly desiring her, even though she couldn't compete outwardly with the glamorous sophisticates who were his usual companions.

He enjoyed her body as much as she enjoyed his.

For long moments she distracted herself remembering his powerful limbs, the curve and dip of his back and taut buttocks, the heavy muscle of his chest. She'd explored his body till he'd pinioned her to the bed with a growl that had awoken every sated nerve. She blushed all over recalling what he'd done then. How she'd delighted in it. So much that she'd cried his name as she'd shuddered in ecstasy.

After Patrick she'd wondered if she'd ever trust a man enough for intimacy. She'd assumed her first time with a man might be clumsy, uncomfortable and nerve-racking.

Instead she felt…treasured. Appreciated. Set free.

The fire in Alaric's eyes had incinerated the doubts and insecurities that had hemmed her in for so long. As if it was right to give in to the passions that simmered below the surface. To trust in herself and him.

He saw beyond her clothes and her job. He was attracted to *her*. He wasn't put off by the fact that she spoke her mind. He even liked her enthusiasm for her work! The news that he'd been intrigued by her right from the start made them seem like equals, despite the disparity in their social positions and experience.

This was true sharing. Something she'd never had.

Bemused, she snuggled into the pillows. If it wasn't for the proof of her exhausted body she'd think it a dream, too good to be true.

Forcefully she reminded herself this wouldn't last.

He was royalty. A tiny chill pierced her glow. He might even be *king*.

Tamsin pulled the bedclothes close as a disturbing thought surfaced. Could that be at the root of her nebulous doubts about Tomas's chronicle? It was the right date. Yet she had doubts.

Doubts or hopes? Selfish hopes that the chronicle was somehow wrong. That Alaric wasn't king.

Because if he became king there was even less chance he'd be interested in plain Tamsin Connors.

Her breath seized on a guilty gasp. Is that why she hadn't told him about the dating? The idea went against every professional principle. Yet deep in her heart a seed of disquiet grew.

Was it so wrong to wait a little to tell him about that? Enjoy this precious interlude before reality intruded?

This…relationship would end soon enough. Her mind shied from the idea of returning to her normal life without Alaric. But he'd given her a wonderful, precious gift. Honest passion and caring, shared unstintingly.

Nothing could ever take that away.

'Ah, Sleeping Beauty awakes.' That deep, rich voice slid like rippling silk right through her insides. Her breath caught at its beauty.

Slowly she rolled over. Backlit by the fire's glow Alaric's long frame was mouth-wateringly athletic in just a pair of black trousers. What was it about a bare male chest, tousled dark hair and a smile that drove sexy creases down his lean cheeks? Tamsin's breath sighed out in a whoosh.

Ink blue eyes met hers and heat trickled in her belly.

'What have you got there?' Her voice was husky and his smile widened. Every doubt fled as its warmth filled her.

He lifted his hand and a splash of fluid gold ran through his fingers. 'Here.' He sauntered to the bed and held up a silken robe.

She reached but he didn't release it, just stood, holding it by the shoulders, wearing a smile of secret challenge. Her gaze flicked to Alaric's bare chest. He had no qualms about nudity, but he was the most magnificent male. Whereas she...she was used to covering up.

His eyes beckoned.

'There's something I want to show you.' When he looked at her that way she felt she could walk across hot coals and feel nothing but the pleasure of his smile.

Shimmying to the edge of the bed she slid out, holding the covers as long as possible. It was stupid to feel shy after what they'd done together. Yet it was only the fact that his eyes remained fixed on her face that gave her courage to step from the bed and slip into the seductively soft silk.

'Excellent.' Why she should feel such pleasure at his approval she didn't want to consider. He smoothed the garment across her flushed skin, wrapping the sides closed across her breasts and stomach, tying the belt and caressing her unashamedly through the sensuous silk.

Her heart beat fast, lodging up near her throat as she sagged into his solid heat. She was exhausted, yet with a touch he overturned every sensible thought. She trembled, eager for his caresses. For more of his loving.

'Come and look.' He ushered her to the window then stood behind her. His arms wrapped around her waist, his body warmed her back and she sank against him.

The sky was dark and the vista almost obliterated by wafts of white. 'A snowstorm?'

His jaw scraped her hair as he nodded. 'We're not going anywhere today.'

Heat blazed and she grinned. Their idyll wasn't over. Yet she tried to be sensible. 'Won't your staff worry? Don't you have appointments?'

'Nothing that can't be delayed. They know we're safe. I texted them before we crossed that last ridge down into this valley. All we can do is wait.'

Tamsin tried to feel regret for Alaric's predicament, cut off from the meetings and important people he dealt with daily. But she couldn't repress a shiver of anticipation.

Before she could guess his intention, he hoisted her into his arms and carried her across the room. No other man had held her like this and she marvelled at the way she fitted so naturally in his embrace.

'We'll have to rough it here,' he murmured.

'Rough it?' The place was pure luxury.

Alaric shouldered open a door into a massive bathroom. The sound of running water made her turn. Set in an arched alcove, lit by flickering candles and topped by a mural of Venus bathing, was the largest bath she'd ever seen. Subtly scented steam curled above it.

On a table nearby were crystal flutes, an ice bucket cradling a foil topped bottle and a plate of plump fresh raspberries and peaches. He must have had the out of season fruit flown in.

'There's only one bath,' Alaric replied. 'I'm afraid we'll have to share.' His eyes gleamed and his roguish smile thrilled as he lowered her, inch by provocative inch to the floor. His hands warmed her hips as she swayed.

Tamsin blinked, overcome by emotion. By the devastating pleasure of this over the top seduction scene. *He'd done this for her.* His darkening gaze invited her to enjoy it all, and him, to the full.

Guilt lanced Tamsin. She should tell him about the chronicle. But with guilt came a renewed sense of urgency. This would be over soon. She knew a bitter-sweet yearning to hoard every precious moment. She'd tell him when they returned to the castle. When the fantasy ended.

She'd never felt so cherished. Invited to share his laughter as well as the passion that lurked in the curve of his lips, his hooded eyes and his tight, possessive grip.

'Thank you, Alaric.' Her voice was hoarse as she stared at this man who'd given her so much. Physical pleasure, but more too. Something that made her feel strong and special.

She stretched up on tiptoe and pressed her unsteady lips to his. Instantly he gathered her close, arms wrapping tightly around her, kissing her with tender persuasion.

Alaric didn't believe in love or commitment. Yet it would be so easy to fall for him. Totally foolish, definitely dangerous, but, oh, so easy.

CHAPTER TWELVE

'No, NOT like that, keep your palm flat.'

Alaric wrapped his hand round Tamsin's, holding it steady while the mare snuffled a chunk of carrot. Tamsin's gurgle of laughter echoed through the stable. He felt it as he stood behind her, his other arm pinning her close.

The horse whickered and mouthed Tamsin's palm. She crooned to it, rubbing her hand along its nose.

Alaric's belly clenched in response to her tone. It was like the one she used when they were naked and he discovered a new erogenous zone on her supple, gorgeous body.

He loved listening to Tamsin, he realised. Whether the soft gasps and cries of delight as they found ecstasy together, or the quiet, serious way she discussed other matters. Or her passion when she talked about books and dead languages and preserving the past. He even liked the schoolmistress voice she used to counter his teasing.

His groin stirred and he tugged her nearer, taking her weight. He was turned on by a woman whose eyes shone with delight over the size of his library!

This was new territory.

Normally his interest in a woman was skin deep. But these past few days with Tamsin he'd discovered a deeper pleasure, sharing her delight, not just with intimacy, but with the world around her.

He'd known joy unfettered by the cold shadows of the past. He even slept soundly, devoid of dreams.

Was it any wonder he didn't want her out of his sight? It was selfish, but the sunshine she brought to his soul was worth ignoring the responsibilities it would be his duty to shoulder soon. Already discreet arrangements were under way to ensure the crown's smooth transition if necessary.

Just a little longer…

A disturbing memory surfaced of Felix talking excitedly about finding the one right woman. *But his brother had made the mistake of believing in love.*

Alaric would never make that error.

'Why are you shaking your head? Aren't I touching it right?'

Alaric rubbed his chin against her hair. 'You *always* touch just right. It's one of your talents.'

Tamsin was a natural sensualist who loved giving and receiving pleasure. Her tentative forays into pleasing him reduced him to a slavering wreck. Imagine when she became expert at seducing a man!

A splinter of dismay punctured his self-satisfaction at the notion of Tamsin sharing herself with another.

Alaric's jaw tensed.

He wouldn't let it happen.

Not yet. Not for a long time. He wouldn't relinquish her until this liaison had run its course.

His left hand crept towards the apex of her thighs.

Her hand clamped his wrist and instantly he felt ashamed. Only an hour ago they'd finally emerged from bed. His attempts to restrain himself, allowing her time to recuperate from their lovemaking, kept failing abysmally. He needed to be more considerate. Until a few days ago she'd never been with a man.

His chest expanded on a rough breath of satisfaction. He couldn't help it. He tried to feel guilty for stealing her virginity but now all he experienced was pleasure knowing he was her first, her only.

It must be the novelty that made him feel he never wanted to let her go.

'Not in front of the horses,' she whispered as he nudged her ponytail aside and kissed her neck.

'You think they'll be offended?' He smiled against her fragrant skin, pulling her back from the stall.

'I…' The word disintegrated in a sigh of delight that stoked his ego.

'You've never been naked in front of a horse?' he teased as he laved her skin.

'I've never been near a horse.' She tilted her head to allow him better access.

'Tragic,' he murmured. 'So much to make up for. Horses, sledding, caviar, breakfast in bed. So many firsts.' He punctuated each word with a tiny bite to her neck and was rewarded by tremors of response that racked her body. He gathered her close. 'What were your parents thinking to deprive you so?'

Did he imagine a stiffening of her slender form?

'I was a very fortunate child. You can't call me deprived.'

No? Alaric thought of how she hid her bright, strong personality behind a dowdy façade. It wasn't a deliberate ploy, he knew now, but part of who she was. He recalled the way her eyes clouded when she'd thought she'd disappointed him. There was a strong streak of self-doubt in his lover and Alaric wished he knew why. With her intelligence and drive it was a wonder she wasn't over-confident.

'Ah.' He nuzzled her hair. 'So you were a pampered miss who got everything her way. All the latest toys on demand?'

She shook her head. 'My parents didn't believe in store bought toys. I amused myself. But I had access to books and solitude to read. I had a secure home and time to dream.'

Alaric's hands stilled in the act of slipping up her ribcage. 'Secure' didn't sound like 'happy'. 'Solitude' had a lonely ring. A familiar ring. His father had ensured Alaric and Felix grew up in impeccable isolation. But at least Alaric had had a brother to look up to.

'What did you dream about, Tamsin?' He cupped her soft breasts and felt her sink against him. 'A prince in a far-away castle?'

'Sometimes,' she whispered.

'Did he have dark hair and blue eyes and his very own sleigh?'

She twisted in his arms. A moment later her arms twined around his neck.

'Of course!' Her eyes gleamed and her lips curved in a gentle smile that tugged at something deep inside.

'What else did you dream about?'

Tamsin shrugged and her gaze dropped. 'I don't know. Adventure. Going out with friends. The usual.'

Alaric thought of the dossier at the castle. It described a girl without siblings or close friends, whose much older parents had busy careers. A girl living a solitary life.

Did she realise how much her words revealed about her loneliness? Something swelled in his chest. Something like pain or regret.

'I think we can organise some adventure.' He tipped her chin and looked into her now guarded eyes. 'We could climb the base of the cliff behind the lodge if it's not too icy.'

Tamsin's eyes lit with golden sparks. Her smile made him feel like royalty in a way he never had before.

'I'd love that! Thank you. When can we go?'

He grinned. He'd *known* she had an adventurous streak. How easy it was to make her happy!

It surprised him how much he wanted her to be happy.

Alaric lifted his hand and pulled her ponytail loose so he could feel her heavy tresses on his hands. He needed this constant connection. To touch and taste, as if he feared she'd vanish if he didn't hold her.

'Another hour to let the sun melt any fresh ice.'

'That gives us time.' Her hands slid down, trailing fire. She yanked his shirt loose and slipped her palms up his torso, flesh against sizzling flesh. His body hardened.

Alaric loved that she was a quick learner.

'Time for what?' His voice was husky as desire twisted in his belly.

'Another first.' Now her smile was mischievous and he felt its impact in some unnamed part of him. 'I've never made love in a stable.'

Heart pounding, Alaric slipped his arms around her and lifted her into his embrace. It felt right. Satisfying.

He turned and strode towards the clean hay in the far corner. 'Allow me to remedy that right now.'

* * *

It was the noise that woke Tamsin. A cry so raw and anguished it made her blood congeal in atavistic terror.

Startled, she lay, breathing deep, wondering what had shattered her slumber. Moonlight streamed through the windows and behind the fire screen embers glowed.

Instinctively she moved closer to Alaric. For the past three days there'd barely been a moment when they weren't touching, even in sleep.

Amazing how she missed that contact.

As she rolled over she realised he was burning up, his skin feverish and damp with sweat.

Tamsin touched his shoulder. It was rigid as if every sinew dragged tight. She leaned close and heard his breathing, sharp and shallow. Her hand slid across his muscled chest that rose and fell in an unnatural rhythm.

'Alaric?'

No response. Did she imagine his breathing was laboured? Desperately she tried to recall everything she'd read about asthma and restricted airways.

'Alaric!' She shook him, alarmed at how her hands slipped on his fever-slickened flesh. 'Alaric. Wake up!' She shook his shoulders.

Restlessly his head turned back and forth. He mumbled something. But try as she might she couldn't wake him.

Fear spiked. They were out of phone range and she couldn't summon help if his condition worsened. Tamsin bit her lip. It wouldn't come to that.

First she had to get his temperature down.

She slid back the covers ready to fetch a damp flannel when another cry rent the air. Her blood froze at the wordless horror of that shout. It tapered into a wail of such grief every hair stood on end.

There was a convulsion of movement. The covers were flung wide and Alaric's hard frame landed on hers with such force it knocked the air from her lungs.

'No!' Huge hands gripped her shoulders. 'You can't!' He choked on the words, his head sinking to her breast.

It took a moment to realise the dampness she felt there wasn't sweat but tears. A sob shook his big body and Tamsin reached up, cradling him close.

'Sh, Alaric.' His distress frightened her, evoking fierce protective instincts. She felt his pain as if it shafted through her body. 'It's all right, darling, do you hear me?' Tamsin squeezed as tight as she could while his shoulders heaved and hot tears smeared between them.

She hated feeling so useless.

She hated that he hurt so badly.

'It's OK. It'll be OK,' she crooned, rocking him as best she could. 'My darling. Everything's all right.'

Gradually, as she murmured endearments, the rigidity seeped from his body and his breathing evened a little.

'Tamsin?'

Still she rocked him, her arms clamped tight. 'It's all right. It was just a dream.'

For long moments he lay still in her arms, then without warning he rolled off her, leaving her bereft.

'Alaric? Are you all right?'

He raised his forearm over his face. In the pallid light she saw his mouth crimp into a stern line as he fought whatever demons plagued him.

Instinctively she moved closer, tugging the discarded bedding to his waist and nestling her head on his chest, one arm wrapped protectively across him. He'd always seemed so strong and confident, so casually in command.

Her distress at his pain was a sharp ache. Was this what happened when you connected with another person? When you shared your true self as well as your body?

'I'm sorry.' His voice was slurred. 'You shouldn't have to witness that.' His breath shuddered out. 'I didn't mean to frighten you.'

For answer she snuggled closer, lifting her leg to anchor his thighs, as if by surrounding him she could blot out his nightmare.

'Don't worry. Everything's fine now.'

'Fine?' The word cracked like a gunshot. 'It'll never be fine.' He tore his arm from his face and she saw his fist pound the other side of the bed. But behind her his arm curved tight, holding her close.

'Did I hurt you?' His voice was a deep rumble. He stared at the top of the four poster bed, as if unwilling to face her. 'Tamsin, are you OK?'

'Of course I'm OK.'

'No questions?' he asked after a minute. 'Surely that enquiring mind of yours wants answers?' His mouth was a grim line in the half-dark.

A month ago his expression would have deterred Tamsin. But now she knew the tender, caring man behind the royal title and the rogue's reputation. She sensed his deep hurt.

She stretched up. Her breasts slid over his chest but she managed to ignore the inevitable tremor of awareness. She leaned over him till her hair curtained their faces in darkness. Holding his jaw in her hands she planted a whisper-light kiss on his lips.

He tasted of salt and heat and suffering.

His mouth was warm beneath hers as she repeated the action, allowing all she felt for him loose in that simple caress. Feelings she hadn't censored.

When she lifted her head one large palm covered the back of her skull and urged her down for another kiss. One so piercingly sweet she ached with the beauty of it. His other arm roped around her hips, drawing her in as if to ensure she wouldn't escape.

As if she wanted to go anywhere!

Never had they kissed like this: a sharing of the soul, not the body. Emotion escalated, filling every lonely part of her. She clung, wanting to explain how she felt but not having the words. Letting her body say what she couldn't.

From nowhere tears welled and spilled unheeded.

'Tamsin?' His thumb stroked her cheek, blurring the hot trail. 'Don't cry. Not over me.'

Too late. She was in too deep. Asking her not to care was like asking her to set fire to a library. Impossible.

Fervently she pressed her lips to his, blotting out whatever he was going to say. He kissed her till she sank into languorous pleasure. Finally he pulled back.

In the dark she felt his gaze. With a sigh he settled her on his chest and wrapped her close. Beneath her ear his heartbeat thrummed steadily.

'I owe you an explanation.' His voice was husky.

'You don't owe me anything. It was just a nightmare.'

'I was selfish, sleeping with you. What if I'd hurt you? I should have let you sleep alone.'

'It's you I'm worried about.' She hesitated, trying to summon an even tone and force away the chill that invaded at the idea of sleeping alone. 'You have these dreams often?'

His silence answered for him.

'You're afraid you might lash out in your sleep?'

'It's too dangerous. I risked your safety.'

'I told you, Alaric, I'm—'

'OK. So you say. But you don't know.' His words tailed off and the desolation she heard cut to her heart. 'Everything I touch turns to ashes. *Everyone.*'

Tamsin froze at the profound despair in his voice.

'Tell me.' She cuddled closer, her mind whirring while she tried to sound cool and detached.

'Talking about it will help?' Sarcasm threaded his voice. She ignored it, guessing he fought deep-seated pain any way he could.

'Bottling it up is no solution.' Look at the way she'd turned inwards, isolating herself rather than take the risk of being rejected. 'Whatever the problem, it will fester if you don't face it.'

'Now you're calling me a coward.' There was a huff of amusement in his voice that made her smile sadly. Alaric was excellent at using humour and his killer charm to deflect attention from the inner man.

How had she not seen it before?

'What have you got to fear? Unless you think I'll do a kiss and tell interview?'

'I can't imagine anything less likely.' He stroked her hair and Tamsin's tension eased a little. She had his trust at least. That was a start.

Silence fell.

'It's not about me,' he said eventually. 'It's the people I failed. That's who I dream of.' He sounded so stern, so judgemental, not like the Alaric she knew.

'I can't imagine you letting anyone down.'

His laugh was bitter. 'Don't you believe it. I was an unruly kid, always in trouble, a constant disappointment to my father. I heard often enough it was lucky I was just a second son. I didn't have what it took to rule.'

Tamsin bit her tongue rather than blurt out that his father sounded like a brute. A man who hadn't loved his wife, or, it seemed, his child. The more she heard the more she disliked.

'Then he'd be surprised to see Ruvingia flourishing now.'

Alaric said nothing. She sensed the reference to his father had been a distraction.

'Alaric? Tell me about your dreams.'

His chest rose beneath her like a wave cresting to shore. Tamsin clung grimly, willing him to share the source of his grief. It ate at him, destroying his peace.

At last he complied. 'I see them all die,' he whispered, 'and I can't save them.'

Tamsin's blood chilled at his haunted tone. 'Tell me.'

'So you can absolve me?' But his scepticism held anguish. Finally when she didn't answer he explained.

As a career army officer he'd jumped at the chance a few years ago to put his skills to good use, volunteering as a peacekeeper overseas. No sooner had he signed on than his whole unit had followed him.

They were posted near an isolated village, protecting a wide area from insurgents. Short bouts of dangerous activity were interspersed with long quiet periods which allowed time to get to know the locals. One little fatherless boy in particular had hung around, fascinated by the foreigners and especially Alaric. From his tone it was clear Alaric had been fond of him too.

When a report came of trouble in an outlying zone Alaric responded immediately, taking men to investigate.

'It was a ruse. But by the time we got there and discovered that it was too late.' They'd returned to their base to discover the village had been attacked. Both soldiers and civilians had been wounded and some had died, the little boy among them.

'He died in my arms.' Alaric's voice was hoarse. 'I couldn't save him.' A sigh racked his body. 'There were too many I couldn't save.'

'There's nothing you could have done.' Her heart broke at the pain ravaging him.

'No?' Glittering eyes clashed with hers. 'I was the officer in charge. If I hadn't split my men the village would have been safe. If I hadn't responded so quickly to an unconfirmed report—'

Tamsin cupped his jaw in her hand. 'You don't know what would have happened. Maybe the attack there would have been worse. You did your best.'

'You don't understand. I was there to protect them and *I failed.* I failed my men too. They were only there because of me. Some didn't survive. Others still bear the scars.' He halted, swallowing. 'Except me. I came home without a scratch.'

Tamsin's heart clenched at the guilt and self-loathing in his voice. She remembered Peter, his livid scar and how he'd talked of Alaric's sense of responsibility. Now it made terrible sense.

'Far better if I'd died too.'

'Don't say that!' Her fist clenched on his chest.

For a moment Alaric let himself enjoy the pleasure of her innocent belief in him. It was novel to have anyone so vehemently on his side.

The whole truth would rip the scales from her eyes. Part of him wanted to keep her in ignorance.

But he didn't deserve her charity.

'I came back to Ruvingia.' He'd been at a loose end, unable to settle, finding it hard to carry out the most routine official duties whilst memories of the deaths plagued him. 'I spent my time amusing myself. Fast cars, parties, women. Lots of women.' Sex had at least brought the oblivion of exhaustion, allowing him to sleep.

'My older brother, Felix, welcomed me.' His gut twisted, remembering Felix's patience with his wayward and tormented younger sibling. 'He was full of plans, even talking of marriage, but I wasn't interested. I was too wrapped up in my own troubles to listen.'

Some days it had been almost too hard to see Felix, so successful, capable and grounded. The epitome of what Alaric had aspired to be but not achieved.

Felix wouldn't have let those he was responsible for die. Felix would have found a way to save them.

'Alaric?'

'There was a girl,' he said, eager now to get this over. 'A beautiful girl. I first noticed her at a function when I saw Felix watching her.' He hefted a breath into tight lungs. 'Two days later she was in my bed.' Another of the stream of women he'd used to lose himself for a while.

Tamsin's body stiffened. Grimly he ploughed on, knowing by the time he'd finished she'd never want to look at him again. He ignored the shaft of pain that caused.

'I didn't love her. I never pretended to. And she… I think my reputation appealed. She wanted the thrill of being with someone notorious.' He grimaced. 'It was mutually satisfying. Till Felix discovered us and I found out she was the woman he'd already fallen for. The one he'd wanted to marry after a proper courtship.'

Tamsin gasped. 'You didn't know?'

'I knew he planned to marry but I assumed it would be an arranged marriage. He hadn't mentioned a name and frankly I wasn't interested.' Alaric paused, forcing out the truth. 'But I knew he was attracted to Diana. Most men were.'

Again he wondered if his pleasure in winning her had been fuelled in part by the need to best Felix. To prove that in this one thing, the ability to get any woman he wanted, Alaric was superior.

Could he have been so shallow? So jealous? What did that say about him?

He'd never before thought himself envious of Felix. But now he couldn't banish telling doubts about his motives.

'Felix was furious when he found out. I'd never seen him like it.' Alaric remembered not only his anger, but his pain. The disillusionment of finding out the woman he'd put on a pedestal had sullied herself with his scapegrace brother. 'He accused us of betraying him.' That memory alone crucified Alaric. Felix was the only person with whom he'd been close. The only person who'd ever really cared.

'And Diana?'

'She was angry she'd made such an error. She hadn't realised he intended marriage. She didn't love him but she liked the notion of being a princess.'

'So what happened?'

Typically, Tamsin was intelligent enough to sense there was more. He let his arm tighten round her soft body, knowing it would probably be for the last time.

'Felix changed. He became short-tempered, not just with me, but everyone. He grew erratic, increasingly unreliable and he began drinking heavily.' The memory of that time, and his inability to stop his brother's slide into depression, chilled Alaric.

'One day I found him climbing into my sports car, determined to drive himself to a function. He reeked of whisky.'

'Oh, Alaric.' Tamsin's palm flattened on his chest and he covered it with his own.

'I couldn't stop him but I couldn't let him go. I jumped in just as he accelerated out of the courtyard.' He drew a deep breath, letting the familiar, corrosive pain claim him. 'We argued.' And each word of Felix's accusations was branded in Alaric's memory, reinforcing every doubt he'd ever harboured about himself.

'Felix lost control on a hairpin bend and I grabbed the steering wheel. We didn't make it around the next curve. We went into the embankment.' His breath grew choppy and sweat prickled his skin. 'I'd buckled my seat belt and the airbag saved me. Felix wasn't wearing his belt. He died instantly.'

Alaric forced himself to relinquish his hold on Tamsin, knowing she'd move away now.

* * *

Tamsin held her breath, shocked at his story. Stunned by the blankness in Alaric's voice. How much he'd suffered! He'd hidden it all behind that charming mask.

It was obvious he'd loved his brother. Given the little she knew, perhaps Felix was the only person who'd ever cared for Alaric.

'I'm so sorry.' The words were pathetically little.

'So am I. Every day. But that doesn't change the fact I'm to blame.'

'Don't say that!'

'If I hadn't seduced Diana, none of it would have happened. If I'd stopped him—'

'If Diana had loved him back, nothing you did could have caused a rift between them.'

There was silence for a moment as if Alaric considered the idea for the first time. Then he shook his head.

'I should have been more careful, less eager to get her into my bed.'

Tamsin couldn't argue with that. 'Your brother blamed you because he was disappointed. It wasn't your fault he loved someone who didn't return his feelings.'

'But he didn't need me undermining him. He deserved my loyalty. I should have been there to help him. Protect him from himself when he turned to drink. I couldn't even do that. *I failed him when he needed me.*' His voice hollowed and Tamsin's throat ached as she stifled tears at his pain.

From the first she'd noticed his tendency to set high standards for himself. Look at the way he'd talked about *taking her virginity.*

Did that overblown sense of responsibility come from being told constantly by his father that his best wasn't good enough? She sensed the weight Alaric bore didn't stem solely from tragic recent events, but from unhealed scars he'd carried a long time.

It didn't surprise her that he wasn't thinking clearly. He'd had one shock piled on another.

Alaric's bitter laughter shredded the silence. 'And here I am, about to take the crown. To do my duty and promise to serve and *protect*! How can I be sure I won't fail again?'

Tamsin's heart broke at his pain and self-doubt. He truly didn't see how capable and competent he was.

No wonder he spent his time dallying with socialites and risking his neck in extreme sports. No wonder he never wanted to be still. He was running from this trauma.

Fury rose in her that those closest to him hadn't seen this. That they hadn't helped him.

Her mind boggled at the weight of guilt he bore. How did he function, much less put on that devil-may-care air? He believed he'd failed his duty to his comrades and his brother. That he was to blame.

That explained why he was appalled at becoming responsible for a nation. And why he didn't want to get close to anyone. He felt himself unworthy. She'd bet, apart from his brother, his comrades were the closest he'd come to a family.

Tamsin breathed out a huff of relief that she hadn't told him the chronicle's date had been verified. Wild horses wouldn't drag that from her now.

'Oh, darling.' She pressed closer, kissing his chin, neck and face. 'You have to forgive yourself. Believe me, you're a victim too.'

He shook his head. 'Tell that to men who came home scarred. Or the mother of an innocent boy who died.'

Tamsin framed his face with her palms. His pain tore at her and she couldn't bear it. 'Your ego is out of control if you think you caused all that! Your brother would be horrified to know you blamed yourself. Do you really think he'd want that? You're a good man, Alaric. I'd trust you with my life.'

'Sweet Tamsin.' He raised a hand and brushed a furious tear from her cheek. 'Don't waste your tears on me.'

'I'll cry if I want to.' He was so stubborn! So eager to shoulder guilt.

Yet his loyalty and honour were part of what made him the man she cared for. *The man she loved.*

Knowledge sideswiped her with a force that left her speechless. Somehow, without her realising, he'd changed from fantasy prince to the man she loved.

Her heart gave a massive jerk and thundered out of control. Her hands shook against his lean cheeks.

She'd thought she risked her pride in coming here, only to discover she'd risked much more.

She'd given her heart to Alaric.

A man with no thought of long term relationships. Who distrusted love. Yet for now even that couldn't dim the incandescent glow filling her.

'We can talk about this later. Now you need sleep.'

'I'll move to another room.'

'Don't even think about it! I'll just follow you.' She slid down into the bed. 'Shut your eyes and rest. I'll stay awake. You won't hurt me.'

'I could get used to you trying to dominate me,' he murmured in a pale imitation of his usual teasing. 'I'm too tired to resist.'

His breath was warm on her skin, his hand splayed possessively at her waist as he tucked her close. But there was nothing sexual about the way they lay. This was about comfort and peace and love.

Even if he didn't believe in it, Tamsin hoped Alaric felt the love drenching her skin, filling her heart, wrapping itself around him.

Later, she knew, her predicament in falling for this man would devastate her. But for now it filled her with a peace she'd never known.

CHAPTER THIRTEEN

THE pink flush of dawn lit the sky as Tamsin crept downstairs. Though Alaric had slept for hours she didn't want to wake him.

She shivered and pulled the silk wrap tighter as she reached the ground floor. The lingering warmth from the central heating made the chill bearable.

Yet nothing dispelled the cold squeezing her heart. How could she even begin to help Alaric?

Or herself. Her situation was impossible.

She was in love.

With Prince Alaric of Ruvingia.

A man with no history of commitment. A troubled man who scorned the notion of falling in love. A man so far beyond her sphere any idea of a relationship was laughable.

Alaric was used to the best in everything. Could he ever settle for someone as ordinary as her? It was ridiculous to hope, but she couldn't stop herself.

Would he ever tie himself to a woman? Especially a woman who wasn't witty or glamorous or well born?

She'd come here knowing she was a short term diversion. At first the bright promise of his offer had been enough. Now she realised she'd been dragged out of her depth.

She loved him.

Tamsin hugged the bitter-sweet knowledge to herself, alternately thrilled and horrified.

Yet as she'd lain, overwhelmed by the realities she faced, part of her brain had pondered the one useful thing she could do: prove once and for all if Tomas's chronicle was legitimate. Lately she'd harboured doubts. Were they well founded or, as she'd begun to suspect, an excuse not to break the news that would take Alaric even further from her?

She thrust open the library door, flicked on the light and headed for the desk. She worked best with pen and paper. Perhaps if she listed her concerns she'd get them straight in her head.

She'd happily give up the kudos of rewriting history with her find if it meant bringing Alaric peace of mind.

He was more important than any professional coup or the chance to rub Patrick's nose in her success. Nothing mattered more than his peace and happiness.

How much had altered these past months!

Despite her selfish fear about the yawning void it would open between them, Tamsin couldn't help regretting that he didn't want the crown. The respect and admiration between Alaric and his people was tangible even if he didn't see it. He'd make an excellent monarch with his dedication to duty and practicality. If only he could see beyond his pain.

She opened a drawer and found a notepad. She withdrew it then paused, an envelope catching her eye.

Tamsin Connors. It was addressed to her?

Her brow puckered as she reached for it. No stamp. No address. Just her name. What did it mean? A trickle of sensation slid down her spine.

'Tamsin!'

Startled, she turned to find Alaric filling the doorway, his face pale and set. Her gaze traversed his perfect, muscular torso and a familiar weakness hit her knees. He wore only jeans, zipped but not buttoned.

No man had a right to look so magnificent! Her pulse gave a queer little leap and hurried on.

'What are you doing?' The hoarse edge to his voice reminded her of his revelations last night. She moved towards him then stopped, uncertain.

'I came to find pen and paper. I had an idea about the chronicle. I wanted—'

'Come back to bed.' He held out a hand, his eyes boring into hers as if to force her to obey. Despite his outstretched hand it wasn't an invitation. It was an order.

'What's wrong?' The room hummed with tension.

'Nothing. I just want you with me. This can wait.' He smiled, but it didn't reach his eyes.

'I'll be up soon,' she assured him. 'I only want to jot some points. Besides, I found this.' She looked at the envelope, frowning as she read her name again.

Before she realised what he intended, Alaric had crossed the room. He stood before her, his palm open as if inviting her to pass the envelope over.

'Leave that. It's not important.' His clipped tone surprised her and she stiffened.

Tamsin looked from those blazing indigo eyes and the stark lines accentuating the stern set of Alaric's mouth to the envelope in her hand. A frisson of foreboding rippled through her. Suddenly the envelope didn't seem quite so innocuous. She wanted to drop it on the desk but her fingers locked tight.

'Why don't you want me to open it?'

Silence. He moved close but didn't touch her. That tiny distance made her feel colder than the chilly dawn air.

'Because it's not for you. It's about you.'

For what seemed an age Tamsin stood, unmoving, staring blankly at her printed name. About her?

Realisation, when it came, rocked her onto her heels.

'You mean an investigation? *Of me?*' For the first time she noticed the date under her name. The day they'd left the castle. Alaric must have brought it with him.

Her head jerked up and their eyes met. His were blank.

Tamsin's heart tripped. She'd grown used to the other Alaric. Warm, generous and fun loving. Caring. She'd almost forgotten the cool control he could summon at will.

'Yes,' he said at last. 'I had you investigated.'

Something squeezed around her lungs and it took a few moments to catch her breath. 'What's in it?'

'I don't know. I haven't read it.'

'Do you have dossiers on every employee?'

It must be a routine security check. But why was it done so recently rather than before she'd come to Ruvingia?

'Not like that.'

Tamsin's heart plummeted. She slipped her finger under the flap and drew out the papers.

Alaric didn't move a muscle. His eerie stillness only increased her fear.

The first page puzzled her. It was about the journalist at the ball. It was only when she turned the page and read a note that there was no evidence of previous contact between him and Tamsin that she understood.

The paper fluttered to the floor.

Other pages were about her and Patrick. Heat rose in Tamsin's cheeks as she recognised office gossip about them. How could Alaric have ordered someone to pry into her life?

'Why didn't you ask, if you wanted to know about the men in my life?' Her mouth twisted bitterly.

Alaric was the only man in her life! Somehow, now, the idea didn't thrill her so much.

'Do you normally vet prospective lovers?'

Alaric shook his head. 'It's not like that.'

'How did you know about Patrick anyway? I didn't mention him to anyone here.' She turned to the last page. What she found turned her heart to a solid lump of ice.

'You had my phone tapped!' She could barely believe it. 'Surely that's not legal, even if you are the prince!'

'It is, if it's a matter of state security.'

'State security! I'm a curator, not a spy!'

'You turned up out of the blue—'

'You invited me here, remember?'

'At a volatile time,' he said as if she hadn't interrupted. 'There's no king. Parliament is in recess till after the coronation, which by law can't take place for several months. It's a time ripe for factions building on past dissension to try toppling the democracy.'

He looked utterly implacable and something inside Tamsin shrivelled. Gone was her tender, vulnerable lover.

'Suddenly you appear, claiming to have proof that I, not Crown Prince Raul, am the legitimate heir. Can you imagine how catastrophic it might be if that news reached the wrong people before we had time to prepare?'

Tamsin stepped behind the desk, needing space to clear her head. Her eyes widened as she saw Alaric's severe expression. The tiny voice that cried this was all a mistake fell silent under the impact of his stare.

'You thought I lied about what I found?' The edges of the room spun as she grappled with the depths of his distrust.

'I acted in the interests of my country.' His tone was stiff, as if he was unused to being challenged.

'You thought that and *still* you took me to bed?'

No, Tamsin. That's why he took you to bed! To distract you, keep you from doing any more damage.

Neutralise the threat. Wasn't that what they called it?

She braced herself against the desk as pain gutted her and she doubled up. Blood roared in her ears like a deafening tide. In a series of snapshots, Tamsin recalled so many tell tale moments.

Her carefully monitored access to the chronicle.

The presence, wherever she went, of staff, no doubt reporting her movements.

Alaric asking her to be his companion, just the day after she'd told him about the chronicle. It had been a ruse, not to keep women away, but to keep an eye on her!

Alaric's fury at the ball when he'd found her with that journalist. He'd lied. He wasn't jealous, just angry she might have revealed something. Or maybe, she thought of what she'd read, Alaric suspected them of being in cahoots.

Pain blurred her vision and cramped her breathing. Her breath sawed in aching lungs as she fought to stay upright.

A hand reached for her and she jerked away.

'Don't touch me! Don't…' She drew an uneven breath. 'I can't bear it.'

To think she'd felt guilty, not telling him immediately about the test results, agonising over whether she could find something to prove or disprove the document once and for all. *And all the time he'd known!*

Her own small omission was nothing compared to his elaborate machinations!

'Tamsin. Have you heard a word I've said?'

'I don't want to hear!' She stumbled to the window, arms wrapped tight around her middle.

'Bringing me here was a ploy, wasn't it?' She stared dry eyed across the snow as cold facts solidified in her shocked brain. 'No wonder the pantry was well stocked. You planned to keep me here, out of harm's way.'

Bitterness scalded her throat. He'd succeeded. For days she'd delighted in the mirage Alaric had created. She'd barely given a thought to her work.

He'd been so sure of her. Had it been a lark, or an unpalatable duty, seducing her?

Tamsin's breath hissed as another piece of the picture slotted into place. The man at the sleigh, handing Alaric an envelope before they left. Alaric's dismissal of her concerns about a change in weather.

'You knew heavy snow was forecast.' She didn't turn. She couldn't face him. Not when the knowledge of her naivety filled her and every breath lanced pain. 'Didn't you? You wanted me cut off here.'

'I knew,' he answered at last, his words dropping like stones into an endless icy pool.

No apology. No regret.

She squeezed her eyes shut. *What they'd shared meant nothing.* Nothing to him but expediency.

It must have galled him to go to such lengths. No wonder he'd been disappointed the first time in that big bed. She hadn't even possessed the skills to please him.

Had he closed his eyes when they'd made love—no, when they'd had sex—and thought of another woman? Someone gorgeous and alluring?

How had she thought, even for one moment, that she'd snared the interest of Alaric, Prince of Ruvingia? Tamsin cringed inside but she kept her spine straight.

'You're an excellent actor.' She ignored the tremor in her voice and stared at the gorgeous alpine vista. 'You had me convinced. Congratulations.'

'Tamsin, it wasn't like that. Not all of it. To start with, yes, I wondered about you. About the way you hid behind that spinster look. About the odds of you finding such a document so conveniently.'

'It wasn't convenient!' She'd spent long hours working in the archives. And all the time he'd thought she'd lied.

'But later it wasn't about the papers, Tamsin.' His voice was nearer, as if he'd followed her to the window. 'It was about how you made me feel. And how you felt.'

'How I felt?' Her fury boiled over and she swung round. 'Are you saying I *asked* you to dupe me? That I *invited* you to make a fool of me?' As she spoke the final, fragile shell of happiness round her heart crumbled.

She'd believed. She'd actually believed in him! How many times before she finally learned her lesson? Was she so imbued with romantic fantasy that she was doomed to fall again and again for men's lies?

Even as she thought it she realised that wasn't possible. She'd survived Patrick's deception but this was far worse. She'd fallen in love with Alaric.

Now she hated him too.

'I'll tell you how this feels, *Your Highness*. It feels like hell! There was no excuse for what you did. None!'

'Tamsin, you have to listen. That's not really why I brought you here.'

She backed away from his outstretched hand as if it were poisoned.

'Not really?' Her voice dripped sarcasm. 'So the phone tap wasn't real? And the goons patrolling the grounds to make sure I didn't meet anyone in secret?' She flung an accusatory hand towards the papers on the floor. 'And the investigator's report—I suppose that was make-believe?'

Did she imagine he stiffened as each accusation lashed like a whip? Or that his face paled beneath its tan?

No! She could afford no sympathy for this man. Already it felt as if she bled from an unseen wound. The sort of injury that would never heal.

'You know what hurts most?' She stood rigidly straight. 'That you discovered how Patrick used me and decided to try the same tactic yourself. And that I fell for it.'

His brow puckered in a marvellous show of apparent innocence. 'I don't follow you.'

'Your report didn't detail that juicy titbit?' She'd skimmed the text, unable to take in every word. 'I don't believe you.' She sucked air to her lungs.

'Patrick set out to make me fall for him. He conned me into helping him *manage his workload* till I found him passing off my work as his. Using it to get a promotion at my expense. When he got it he dumped me and took up with a sexy blonde who knew how to please a man.' She almost gagged, remembering Patrick's satisfaction as he'd said that.

'And now you, you…' She blinked dry, scratchy eyes. 'I can't believe I fell for it again. That I actually *believed* you were attracted to me.'

She couldn't go on. Bile rose in her throat and her stomach churned queasily. Being sick in front of Alaric would be the final humiliation.

Tamsin stumbled to the door, thrusting aside his hand, ignoring his call for her to stop as pain, nausea and despair took hold.

The cold seeped into Alaric's bones as he stood, staring at the library's empty fireplace. It wasn't the chill air that froze his half-dressed body. It was the memory of Tamsin's distress. *The pain he had caused.*

Guilt flexed its claws, raking his belly. Lacerating the peace he'd discovered these past days with Tamsin.

Seeing her anguish, hearing her desperate attempt to keep her voice steady, Alaric had wanted to gather her close and comfort her. Force her to accept his embrace. Accustomed as he was to causing pain, he couldn't bear this.

Letting her leave had been the ultimate test of endurance when every instinct roared for him to go to her.

Yet he had to give her time alone. Enough to calm a little so she'd listen.

She felt betrayed by him.

He turned to pace, unable to remain inactive. If only he'd known her history with the Englishman! How much more damage had Alaric done to her bruised self-esteem?

She thought he'd used her for his own ends too.

But it hadn't been like that.

Yes, he'd been selfish. He'd seduced an innocent. But his motives, though not pure, hadn't been as despicable as the Englishman's. Her work had been a catalyst for intimacy. Yet it had also provided a convenient excuse. How much easier to explain away his fascination with a drably dressed bookworm than admit she intrigued him? That he wanted her in ways he'd never wanted anyone? Ways that had as much to do with emotions as with sexual gratification?

Air punched from his lungs as an unseen blow pummelled his solar plexus.

Emotions.

He'd spent so long distancing himself from intimacy except the sort he found in the beds of accommodating women. It was a shock to realise how much he felt for Tamsin. How much he *cared.* He'd thought it impossible, but it was true.

Instantly fear rose. Its familiar, hoary hand clenched his heart and iced his blood. No matter how he fought he couldn't blot out the voice in his soul.

He tainted everyone he touched.

He should never have allowed himself near Tamsin, so bright and generous and trusting.

His darkness spread like a miasma, infecting everyone he cared for. Now it had soiled that brief bright moment of delight. It had engulfed Tamsin too. He'd let her down.

But how to look into her bright eyes and listen to her soft, serious tones and not give in to temptation? For all his inner darkness, he was a man, not a machine. Resisting her innocent sweetness, her tart asperity and her zest for living had been impossible.

He'd craved an end to the darkness and he'd got that from her. No wonder he'd been insatiable, unable to bear her out of his sight. Before her his smiles and banter had carefully masked bleak emptiness. She'd filled that void with light and warmth.

Alaric recalled her soft murmurings as she'd listened to his story. Instead of shunning him when she'd heard what he'd done she'd called him 'darling' as naturally as if it might even be true. The sound of it had lodged somewhere near his heart and he'd cherished it.

He'd be damned if he'd give that up.

Twenty minutes since he'd let her walk away. A sensitive man might wait longer before confronting her. But his need was too urgent. He strode from the room.

The turret bedroom was empty. Alaric refused to think of it as *their* room, though the hint of her scent and the sight of rumpled sheets hit him in the chest like a ton of bricks. Setting his jaw, he searched the other rooms. Empty.

Fear ratcheted up in his belly.

It was only as he paused by a window that he realised where she'd gone. Her tracks led to the cliff where he'd given her a climbing lesson.

His heart almost failed as he remembered telling her that was the quickest way to the castle. It was an easy climb if you were experienced, but for a novice…

He'd hurt her so badly she'd rather face the mountain than him?

Alaric was no stranger to anguish but as he raced downstairs his torment was worse than anything he'd known.

If anything happened to her…

The cold numbed Tamsin's hands as she trudged through the snow. She'd forgotten her gloves in her haste but she wouldn't return for them. Not yet. Not till she'd found the strength to face Alaric without crumbling in a heap.

The nausea had eased a little but the pain was so raw, so sharp, she could barely breathe.

She shoved her hands in her anorak pockets and averted her eyes from the place where he'd taught her to climb. He'd been so tender and patient.

A sham!

Quickening her step she passed the small cliff and came to the base of a steep mountain slope. She'd have no trouble retracing her steps but for now she wanted solitude.

If she could she'd run away and never face him again.

The thought made her stumble to a halt.

She'd run across Europe rather than face Patrick. She'd spent years hiding herself rather than risk the chance of rejection. She'd thought there was strength in independence. But she hadn't been independent. She'd been a coward.

If she were truly the new, independent woman she'd been so proud of the night of the ball, she'd face Alaric.

She was furious and hurt by how he'd used her. But almost as bad was knowing she'd made the same mistake again. Fooled twice by manipulative men. Only this time her mistake was irredeemable. She'd fallen for Alaric, heart and soul. Despite his ruthless actions he was so much more than the flawed man he thought himself.

Something, an awareness, made her turn. An hour ago the sight of Alaric chasing her through the snow would have thrilled her, a precursor to some new lovers' game.

Now it was despair she felt, for even knowing how he'd used her, her heart leapt at the sight of him. Her blood roared in her ears. Would she always react to him like this?

'Run!' He was so near she saw his eyes blaze fire.

For a moment she saw stark fear in those glittering depths, then his hands closed on her and she was running, stumbling, carried by the force of his charging body. He kept her on her feet, urging her, tugging her at an impossible speed through the snow.

It was only as he spoke again that she realised the whispering roar wasn't her blood. She saw his lips move but the sound was obliterated by the thunder of tonnes of snow and rock falling off the mountain.

Avalanche! She read his lips but it was his urgent hands, his grim expression, that gave her strength to run.

Ahead a curve in the line of the mountain promised safety. They couldn't possibly make it. Then with a tremendous shove at her back Alaric propelled her forward.

She sprawled, hands over head as snow and scree dropped around her. The thud of the avalanche reverberated through the valley, snapping her teeth together. But the fall here on the periphery of the slide was relatively light.

Finally it was over. Gingerly she moved, burrowing her way up, grateful for the sight of sky above. She dragged in a deep breath scented with pine and ice and adrenaline.

Without Alaric she would have been buried under the massive fall. She turned to thank him.

To find only a huge tumbled mass of ice and boulders.

CHAPTER FOURTEEN

'THE prince is being released from hospital.' Tamsin's colleague gave her a sidelong glance. 'He'll be back at the castle soon.'

'That's excellent news.' Tamsin pinned on the cool, professional smile she'd perfected. It concealed the fluttery reaction in her stomach at the mention of her employer, her ex-lover. The man she dreamt of every night. 'I didn't think he'd be out so soon.'

After fracturing his collarbone, a leg and an arm, as well as sustaining concussion, the pundits had said Alaric would be under medical supervision far longer.

'Apparently the doctors didn't want to release him but he refused to stay any longer.'

Tamsin nodded, remembering Alaric's determination and strength. He had so little regard for himself he'd probably ignored medical warnings. A twinge of worry stabbed her. Would he be all right?

She still got chills thinking of those long minutes as she'd scrabbled beneath the debris to the seemingly lifeless form she'd finally found. Her heart had plunged into freefall as she'd searched for a pulse.

In that moment it didn't matter how he'd used her, how he'd cold-bloodedly taken her into his bed. All that mattered was that she loved him and he might die.

It had felt like *her* life blood oozing across the snow.

The metallic taste of fear filled her mouth as memory consumed her. Her helplessness, till she'd found Alaric's mobile phone and, miracle of miracles, discovered it still functioned. She'd felt only a desperate satisfaction that, despite what he'd led her to believe, there was perfect phone reception. Within twenty minutes medical staff had arrived by helicopter.

'Perhaps he'll visit the archives to see how we're getting on.' No missing her colleague's arch tone of enquiry. Not surprising given Alaric's previous impromptu visits.

But he'd only come because he didn't trust her.

Had he fretted all those weeks in hospital, wondering if she'd talked of what she'd found? The surveillance seemed to have stopped. She'd lost the claustrophobic sense of being watched.

'I suspect the prince has more important things to do.'

Even she had heard the speculation about Crown Prince Raul's delay in finalising his coronation, and how much time he spent closeted with his injured cousin. No doubt they were organising for Alaric to be crowned when he recovered.

He'd make an excellent monarch. Stoically she ignored the fact that his coronation would hammer the final nail in the coffin of her wishful dreams. Dreams that even his actions hadn't quite managed to stifle.

Tamsin looked at her watch. 'Time to pack up, don't you think?' She ignored her companion's curious look. For well over a month she'd faced down blatant interest about her relationship with Alaric.

Only when she was alone in the room did she slump in her chair, her heart pounding at the thought of Alaric here, in the castle again.

His pain still haunted her. Her heart ached for him and all he'd been through. Once she'd believed she could help him. As if *she*...

She bit her lip. She'd done with fantasy.

These past weeks had been a hell of worry about Alaric and constant scrutiny from the curious. Yet she'd endured. She'd put up with the gossip and completed the initial period of her contract, determined to fulfil her obligation.

Did her resolve stretch to seeing him again?

Tamsin shot to her feet, too edgy to sit. They'd find someone to replace her when she didn't renew her contract. Patrick perhaps. Strangely she felt no qualms about the idea of him here in what had been her territory.

She wouldn't return to Britain. But there'd been that offer last year of a job in Berlin, and a hint about work in Rome. She'd delayed following up either opportunity. Her lips twisted as she realised it was because in her heart she wanted to be close to Alaric.

Pathetic! There was nothing to stay for. The sooner she moved on the better. Starting with a weekend in Berlin or Rome. Either would do.

Would it be easier to heal a broken heart in new surroundings?

Out of nowhere pain surged, cramping her body and stealing the air from her lungs. It took a full minute to catch her breath and move again.

Tamsin refused to acknowledge the fear that nothing would heal what ailed her. She felt a terrible certainty that the love she still felt for Alaric, despite everything, would never be 'healed'.

'The answer is still no.' Alaric hobbled across the hospital room. He set his mouth against the pain when he moved too fast. 'I won't do it. That's final.'

'Do you think I liked the idea of an arranged marriage, either?' Raul sounded weary. They'd been over this time and again. 'It's your duty, Alaric. If you accept the crown then you accept the responsibilities that go with it.'

'Don't talk to me of duty!' Alaric's clenched fist connected with the wall but he barely felt the impact. 'I don't want this, any of it. I'm only accepting the crown because, like you, I've been brought up to do my duty.'

Strange how things had changed since the accident. His fear of failure had dimmed. He no longer got that sick feeling in his belly at the thought of ruling the nation. He could face the idea of leadership again with equanimity, though being monarch wasn't his choice.

In hospital he'd had plenty of time to think. To his surprise he'd realised how much he'd enjoyed the work he'd begun in Ruvingia. It had been satisfying solving problems and organising innovative community renewal. He'd like to follow through the improvements they'd begun in his own principality.

But as king he couldn't be so hands on. His life would be all protocol and diplomacy.

At least he knew now he could face what was required of him.

What had changed? Even the nightmares had receded a little. Because he'd broken the curse of good luck that had seen him emerge unscathed from tragedy? Because he'd shattered his body and almost lost his life, proving his mortality? No, it couldn't be that simple.

He'd been overwhelmed by the genuine distress of his people after the accident. The number of communities and groups who'd sent representatives had stunned him. They'd wished him well, and, as he recovered, sought his renewed input to their projects.

Yet Alaric knew the real change had come from his brief glimpse of happiness. The peace and sense of connection he'd felt in his short time with Tamsin. Surely that's what had hauled him back from the brink of self-destruction, giving him hope for the first time in years.

Six months ago he'd have embraced death with equanimity. But lying in hospital as doctors fussed over him; Alaric had discovered he wanted to live so badly he could taste the need.

He *had* to live, to see Tamsin and set things right.

The night he'd shared his past with her had cracked something wide open inside him. Not just his guilt and fear. But a lifetime of barriers. Barriers that had kept him cut off from love, preventing him building a real relationship.

'Alaric.' His cousin's voice yanked him from his reverie. He turned and met Raul's sympathetic look. 'I know this is hard on you.'

'Hard on us both.' Raul had been raised to be king. It was a measure of his integrity that he'd taken so well the stunning news that Alaric should be monarch. The final testing and double checking of Tamsin's document and other contemporary sources had proven her right. Alaric was destined to be king, not Raul.

Raul shrugged. 'There's no way out of the wedding. You think I haven't double checked? It's a binding agreement. The Crown Prince of Maritz is betrothed to marry the Princess of Ardissia. No negotiation.'

'Even though we don't know where she is?' If Alaric had his way they'd never locate her.

'We will soon. And when we do…' Raul shrugged.

'A royal wedding.' A loveless marriage. Surely the only sort he wanted or deserved. Yet his blood froze.

He remembered Tamsin's smile, felt the radiant warmth it brought his blighted soul. He heard her soft cries of delight as he pleasured her, smelled her fresh summer scent.

She hadn't come near him since the accident. She *hated* him for what he'd done to her.

His chances of persuading her to forgive him were slim.

But to marry another woman…

Alaric stiffened, realising there was only one way forward. It would be perhaps the most difficult thing he'd ever done, but he had no choice.

'I *beg* your pardon?' Tamsin couldn't believe her ears.

'None of the documents held in safekeeping can be released without His Highness's permission.' The secretary sounded uncomfortable.

'But it's *my* passport!' Tamsin shot to her feet, the phone pressed to her ear, then drew a calming breath. 'There must be a misunderstanding. The passport was held for safekeeping only.'

'You're planning to travel?'

Tamsin frowned. She shouldn't have to report her plans. But maybe it would stir this bureaucrat into action.

'I fly to Rome this weekend.' An overnight trip to discuss a possible job. She told herself she'd be enthusiastic about it once she got to the sunny south. 'So when can I collect it?'

Another pause. 'I'll have to get back to you on that. The prince gave specific instructions…'

A chill fingered its way down Tamsin's spine. *Alaric's* instructions? Impossible! He couldn't want her here.

Yet he'd manipulated her before. Was it possible he was doing it again? Fury sparked. She would *not* be a pawn in his games again.

The secretary was talking when she dropped the phone into its cradle.

Fifteen minutes later Tamsin entered the royal antechamber. Ironically she'd made it through security easily. Chancing to meet the servant who'd come to fetch Alaric the night of the ball, she'd asked for directions, letting him believe Alaric had sent for her.

As she entered the room a man, busy at a desk, looked up.

'The prince is not receiving visitors.'

Tamsin's eyes narrowed as she recognised his voice. The secretary who'd stonewalled her on the phone.

'This can't wait.' She kept walking.

'Wait!' His eyes flicked to the double doors on the other side of the room. 'If you take a seat I'll check the prince's schedule.'

Her pace quickened. She was sure now that Alaric was in the next room. Tamsin wasn't about to be fobbed off. Whatever was going on she'd get to the bottom of it. Now.

'Thank you. But I'll make my own appointment.'

From the corner of her eye she saw him scramble to his feet, but he was too late. She wrenched open the door and catapulted through it, her heart pounding as adrenaline surged. She'd hoped to avoid confronting Alaric again, yet part of her longed to see him one last time.

Two steps into the room she stumbled to a halt, eyes widening at the tableau before her. Alaric was there but so were many others, all formally dressed and wearing sober expressions. There was a sprinkling of uniforms, clerical robes and a few judges in old-fashioned costumes.

In the centre sat Alaric, one arm in a sling, writing at a vast desk. He put his pen down and looked up.

Lightning blasted her senses as his piercing eyes met hers down the length of the chamber. Her body quivered with the impact of that look.

Tamsin swayed and shut her eyes, aghast at her weakness. She had to get away from him once and for all. Going to Rome was the right thing.

A hand grabbed her elbow. 'My apologies for the intrusion, Highness.' The hand tugged and Tamsin opened her eyes.

The secretary's words had made everyone present turn to look. Silence reigned for a moment and despite crawling embarrassment she stood straight, facing the curiosity of the gathered VIPs.

What had she stumbled into?

'It's all right.' Alaric's voice drew her gaze to where he sat, so handsome in dress uniform. 'Dr Connors is my welcome guest.' Did she imagine his voice deepened seductively?

No! There was nothing between them. There never had been. She had to remember that.

'Of course, Your Highness.' The man released her, bowed and melted away.

Silently Alaric gestured her to a chair and she went to it gratefully. Yet she didn't sit. By now she knew she'd interrupted something important. The judges stepped forward with deep bows and signed the document Alaric passed to them. Then several others, all with a slow formality that proclaimed this a significant occasion.

Finally Alaric stood. Tamsin's heart clenched as he limped from his chair. He was pale, his face pared down. She wanted to smooth her palm across his face, trace the high slant of his cheekbone and reassure herself he was all right. Her hands trembled with the force of what she felt.

The day of the accident she'd stayed as close as she could, scared to let him out of her sight till finally the doctors pronounced him out of danger. Since then she hadn't seen him, knowing it was better that way. Yet she'd scoured the news reports for updates on his recovery.

He must have come here straight from the hospital.

Anyone else seeing his straight backed stance would think him fully recovered. But to Tamsin's eyes there was a stiffness around his neck and shoulders and a tension in his jaw that betrayed pain.

What was so important he'd left the hospital for it? Couldn't anyone else see he needed rest?

Impotent anger surged. It was no use telling herself he didn't need her sympathy. She couldn't squash her feelings.

Alaric turned to the man beside him. A tall, handsome man with familiar features. Alaric said something she couldn't hear and bent his head in a bow. But before he could complete the action the other man spoke sharply and put a hand on Alaric's shoulder.

Alaric raised his head and for a moment Tamsin saw something flash between the two. Wordless understanding. Then Alaric spoke, making his companion laugh and reach to shake his hand vigorously.

There was a burst of applause and cheers in Ruvingian that Tamsin wished she understood. The two men turned to face their audience, accepting the accolade with an ease that spoke of long practice.

She watched Alaric avidly. This might be the last time she saw him and she wanted to imprint every detail. The way he smiled. The light in his eyes as he nodded at something his companion said. Familiar hunger swamped her. It was like watching a feast through a window and knowing though you were starving you couldn't reach out and eat.

Instead she tasted the ashes of hopeless dreams on her tongue.

At a word from Alaric, the crowd began to leave. They were too well bred to stare, but she felt their surreptitious glances. Heat gathered in her cheeks but she stood her ground. She wasn't into hiding any more.

Last to leave was the tall man who'd stood with Alaric. He too was in his early thirties. He wore his hand-tailored suit with an easy elegance that might have made her stare if she hadn't been so conscious of Alaric behind him.

'Dr Connors.' The stranger lifted her hand to his lips in a courtly gesture that would stop most feminine hearts. Over his shoulder she caught Alaric's sharp stare and fire sparked in her veins.

'It's a pleasure to meet you. I'm Alaric's kinsman, Raul.'

Tamsin blinked and focused on the man who she now saw bore a striking resemblance to Alaric. Jade green eyes instead of indigo and a leaner build, but the same angled cheekbones, strong jaw and lush dark hair. The same indefinable air of power and authority.

'Your Highness.'

He smiled, unfazed by the tension emanating from his cousin's rigid form. Tamsin could feel it from where she was but Prince Raul merely released her hand slowly. 'I'll look forward to our next meeting.'

Then he was gone. She was alone with Alaric.

CHAPTER FIFTEEN

'HELLO, Tamsin. It's good to see you.'

Alaric's voice was low and smooth, evoking memories of heady passion and soft endearments. In that moment her indignation bled away, replaced by longing and regret.

'Hello, Alaric.' Her voice was breathless, as if she'd run across the castle compound and up four flights of stairs instead of being escorted in a state of the art lift.

Silence fell as their eyes locked. Tamsin wanted to look away but couldn't, mesmerised by something in his gaze she'd never seen.

Despite the sling and a slight limp as he walked towards her, Alaric was a formidable figure: handsome, virile and powerful. Tamsin's nerves stretched taut as she fought not to respond to his nearness. Yet her stomach filled with butterflies and her knees trembled.

If only she couldn't remember so clearly the bliss she'd found in his arms.

But seeing him at the centre of that gathering, easily dominating the proceedings, had reinforced everything she'd told herself the last six weeks or so. That they belonged to different worlds.

'What was that, just now?' Jerkily she gestured to the desk where so many people had come forward to sign that large parchment. 'Some sort of ceremony?'

'Royal business,' he said, watching her so intently it seemed he noted every move, every expression. Was he wondering how he'd brought himself to make love to her?

Heat rushed into her cheeks. When he didn't explain further, Tamsin understood. His silence reinforced that she had no business enquiring into matters of state. The gulf between them was unbreachable.

He seemed taller, looming over her, making her feel vulnerable. His eyes were darker. They looked almost black. Try as she might she couldn't read his shuttered expression.

He stepped near and instantly her nerve ends tingled in awareness. Automatically she inched back a step, then, realising what she was doing, planted her feet.

'How are you, Alaric?'

'As you see.' His lips twisted ruefully. 'I survived.'

'Will you recover fully?' She gestured to his stiff leg.

'I'm told so.'

Her heart thudded in relief and she clasped her hands, unable to tear her gaze from those unfathomable eyes.

'It's my fault you were injured—'

'Don't even *think* of apologising!' The words shot out like bullets. He leaned towards her, his eyebrows lowering like storm clouds over flashing eyes.

'I'm the one who's sorry.' His mouth flattened. 'I tried earlier, at the lodge, but you wouldn't accept my apologies.'

Tamsin frowned. She couldn't remember that. But the scene was a blur of misery and grief.

He shifted as if it pained him to stand. 'I had no business seducing you. You are a guest in my country, an employee.'

Tamsin didn't know why her heart shrivelled at his reminder of their relative stations. It was true yet for a bright brief period it hadn't seemed to matter. That had been an illusion. Part of his seduction technique.

'I should never have—'

'Please!' She couldn't bear him to go on, enumerating everything that had happened between them. She'd relived every moment these past weeks and it brought no solace, just aching regret like a cold lump of lead in her chest.

'Don't go on. I accept your apology.' She turned to face the glowing fire in the ornate fireplace rather than meet his intense gaze. 'You believed you were protecting your country.'

It had taken her a long time but finally she'd seen a little of his perspective. A perspective reinforced by the scene she'd just witnessed. He had responsibilities for a nation that weighed heavily.

Tamsin understood his motives but that didn't excuse his tactics. She cringed at the thought of others listening to her conversation with Patrick. And as for Alaric letting her think he really cared, really desired her…

'You're very forgiving.'

She avoided his eyes. 'I've had time to consider.'

'But there's no excuse for—'

'No, but I don't want to discuss it.' Pain clawed at her. She didn't want to revisit the details. Like how he'd bedded her as part of his scheme. Or how she'd given her heart to him.

At least he didn't know that. How much more sorry for her he'd be if he knew she'd fallen in love.

Listening to his mellow baritone was delicious torture. Being here with him was what she'd dreamed of and yet it was dangerous.

She wanted what she could never have. She'd fallen for an illusion, believing in a relationship that could never be. Pain seeped from her cracked heart.

'You saved me the trouble of coming for you.'

At his words her head jerked round. Alaric had intended to come for her? For a foolish instant hope quivered in her heart, only to be dashed by harsh reality. No doubt he'd planned to deliver his apology and suggest she leave, rather than stay and embarrass them both.

'I've come for my passport.' The words came out full of strident challenge.

Did she imagine a stiffening of his tall frame?

'You want to leave?' He frowned.

'Yes!' How could he even ask it? 'But I need my passport and I'm told I need your permission to get it.'

'What if I asked you to stay?' His eyes probed, laser bright.

'No!' Her response was instantaneous. He couldn't be so cruel as to expect her to remain. Seeing him, always from a distance, would be unbearably painful.

A sound broke across her thoughts and she looked up. Alaric's mouth had twisted up at one side.

Surely he wasn't laughing at her?

Indignation and fury warred with hurt. A voice inside protested Alaric would never be so deliberately cruel. He wasn't callous like Patrick.

But she knew to her cost men *were* cruel.

She spun on her foot and marched to the door. She'd get a lawyer to retrieve her passport.

Tamsin was reaching for the door handle when something shot over her shoulder. A hand slammed onto the door, holding it shut. Alaric's arm stretched in front of her and her skin prickled at how close he stood. His heat was like a blaze at her back.

'No!' The single syllable cracked like a gunshot. 'You're not leaving. Not like this.'

Alaric's chest ached as he forced himself to drag in oxygen. His pulse thundered, pumping adrenaline through his body. The sight of Tamsin storming out of his life had been impossible to bear.

'I refuse to stay and be the butt of your humour.'

He stared at her glossy hair, her slim shoulders and lithe body and felt heat punch his belly. She thought he'd laughed at her?

'Tamsin, no. It's not like that.' It had been more a grimace of pain than anything else. Pain that slashed bone deep. 'If I was laughing it was at myself.'

'I don't understand.' She didn't move a muscle, but neither did she try to wrestle the door open.

'I told Raul I was going to ask you to stay. I was just remembering his response.'

'You talked to your cousin about me?'

She turned, looking up with wide amber-gilt eyes that melted his bones. He shuddered with the effort of controlling the emotions threatening to unravel inside.

'He thought I'd have no trouble persuading you. Then, as soon as I suggested it, you instantly objected.' Objected! *She'd turned ashen. As if she couldn't think of anything worse than being with him.*

Fear petrified him, as strong as in that soul-wrenching moment when he'd seen her in the path of the avalanche.

What if he couldn't persuade her? Had he hurt her so much he'd destroyed his last tentative hope?

He refused to countenance the thought.

'I don't understand.' She blinked and looked away, as if she couldn't bear to look at him. He didn't blame her.

His self-control splintered. He lifted his hand, stroking knuckles down her velvet cheek. His fingers hummed as a sensation like electricity sparked beneath his skin. She gulped and a tiny fragment of hope glowed in the darkness of his heart.

'I don't want you to leave. I won't allow it.' He cupped her chin and lifted her face till she had no option but to meet his gaze. The jolt of connection as their eyes clashed shook him to the core.

'You have no right to talk about allowing.' The belligerent set of her jaw spoke both of pain and strength. His heart twisted as he recognised one of the things that drew him to her was her indomitable spirit.

'No. I have no right.' The pain of these past weeks returned full force. 'But I'm too selfish to give up. *I'll make you stay.* Whether I have to persuade you or seduce you or imprison you in the highest tower.' Her lips parted in shock. The urge to kiss her soft mouth was almost more than he could bear.

'You're crazy.' She stepped away, only to back into the door. Alaric paced forward till a hair's breadth separated them. Tamsin drew a strained breath and the sensation of her breasts brushing against him made him groan. It had been so long since he'd held her. Too long since he'd kissed her.

'No!' She held him at bay.

She didn't want him after what he'd done.

'Tamsin, I…' He hesitated, groping for words to express unfamiliar feelings. Feelings he hadn't believed in before her.

'Let me go, Alaric.' She looked away, blinking. 'I don't know what new game this is but I've had enough.'

'Sh, darling, I know.' Gently he brushed a strand of hair off her face, his heart twisting as she flinched from his touch. But he couldn't resist tracing the line of her throat down to the pulse hammering at her collarbone.

'It's not a game. It's gone far beyond that. Once, in my complacency, I planned to seduce you.' Pain wrapped gnarled fingers around his heart as he read her anguish.

'I told myself it was for the benefit of the nation I kept you close, kept you with me, even kidnapped you.' He drew a breath that racked his body. 'But from the start I lied, not just to *you* but to myself. I plotted to get you into my bed *because I wanted you.* I needed you as I've never needed anyone. I couldn't stop thinking about you. Not your chronicle and your news about the throne, but you.'

He tunnelled his good hand through her hair, revelling in its silk caress and the warmth of her close to him. For the first time since the accident he felt *complete.*

'You don't know how I've missed you.' His voice was a hoarse groan and her eyes riveted to his. He was drowning in warm, amber depths.

'I fell for you, Tamsin. That's why I kidnapped you. The rest was an excuse.' She shook her head but he pressed on. 'At first you were a problem with your unwanted news. But you were a conundrum, too, a woman I couldn't get out of my head. You intrigued me. I've never met anyone like you.'

'Because I'm a misfit, is that it?' Her eyes shimmered, overbright.

'You? A misfit? The way you charmed ambassadors and aristocrats and commoners alike at the ball? The way you bonded with those teenagers at the community centre? I hear you've kept visiting and they love it. And your staff in the archives have nothing but admiration and liking for you.'

'You've been spying on me again?'

'No!' It had gone against the grain the first time. He'd never do that again. 'Their permanent employer wants them back and they petitioned my staff to remain. While you stay they want to.'

He watched her eyes widen. She genuinely had no idea how special she was with her talents, her intellect and above all her passion.

'I used every excuse I could think of to keep you with me, Tamsin. But the truth is I did it all because I wanted you.' Even though he didn't deserve her, he was too selfish to let her go.

'I still want you. I need you.' Saying it aloud for the first time Alaric was stunned by the force of his emotions. Emotions he'd never thought to experience. Emotions strong enough to obliterate a lifetime's cynicism.

She shook her head so vigorously her hair came down to swirl like a dark cloud around her. He wanted to bury his face in it, inhale her sweet scent and lose himself.

But her pain, like a razor wire fence between them, held him back.

'I'm a novelty. A change from your sophisticated women.' Bitterness laced her voice. 'You don't need me.'

'You *are* different.' He reached for her hand and planted it over his chest, pressing it to his pounding heart. 'For the first time in so long I *feel*, Tamsin. It scared the life out of me. That's why I kept telling myself it wasn't real.'

'No!' Her shout startled them both. 'Please, don't. This isn't real. You feel guilty, that's all.'

Alaric looked into Tamsin's taut features, searching for a softening, some proof she cared. But there was nothing, only pain. The tiny flame of hope flickered perilously and his chest hollowed.

Had he lost his one chance of happiness?

'I love you.' He swallowed and it was like every broken dream scored his throat. He'd never thought it possible to feel so much and it scared him as nothing ever had.

'I realised that as I lay in hospital and replayed every mistake I'd made. That's why I signed myself out early, to come and tell you. *I love you.*'

She stood like a statue, her brow furrowed and her mouth a tight line.

He'd never felt like this, never told any other woman he loved her.

He'd expected a better response!

Alaric was tempted to kiss her into compliance. He could win her body. Yet he wanted her mind too. Her heart.

'You don't believe me?'

'I…don't know. It seems so unlikely.' She looked so dazed his heart squeezed in sympathy. Or was that fear?

'Then believe this. That scene you walked in on? I wanted it over before I came to you today.' His lips twisted, thinking how Tamsin always managed to turn his plans on their head. 'The reason for all the witnesses was because I wanted there to be no question about my actions.' He drew a slow breath and squeezed her hand. 'I just signed away my claim to the throne of Maritz. Raul will be king after all.'

'You did *what*? Oh, Alaric! You'd make a wonderful king. You mightn't be able to see it but I can. And I'm not the only one. The—'

He silenced her with a finger on her lips, telling himself soon he'd feel their soft caress with his mouth.

'It's all right, Tamsin. I didn't do it because I feared to take the throne.' That was well and truly behind him, though it warmed him to have her as such a passionate advocate. Hope flared again and excitement sizzled in his bloodstream.

'I discovered the king is obligated to marry a princess from Ardissia. I'd have to take on the throne and a ready-made wife. When it came to the crunch I couldn't do it. I'd accept the kingship and all its responsibilities but I can't marry another woman. Not when I love you.'

'*You did that for me?* You hardly know me!'

'I know you, Tamsin. I know the real you.'

He'd never known a lovelier woman.

He looked down into her stunned face. Her hair was loose around her shoulders. Her intelligent eyes were bright, her skin glowed and the delicate curve of her cheek made him want to stroke her till she purred. She wore a fitted russet suit he'd never seen before. It skimmed her curves in a way that made his hormones rev into high gear.

'You've bought new clothes.' He frowned. He wasn't sure he wanted her looking good for anyone but him.

'You really abdicated?' She cut across him, staring as if she'd never seen him before. 'But that's…'

Her lips curved in a tremulous smile that snared his heart all over again and sent heat scudding through every tense muscle. 'I can't believe you gave up a crown for me.'

'In the end it wasn't the crown I objected to.' He hauled her close with one arm, his pulse racing. 'It was the bride. I prefer to choose my own.'

Cool palms slid around his neck as she pressed close, her eyes a blaze of molten gold. It was like staring into the sun. Surely she couldn't look at him like that and not…

He took his courage in his hands.

'Tamsin, could you forget the past and start again?'

For what seemed an age she stood silent. He held his breath.

'I don't want to forget,' she murmured. 'You've given me so much.' Her smile warmed every corner of his soul and his pulse tripped into overdrive.

'Tamsin.' His voice was so husky he had to clear his throat. 'Could you live with a man who's made mistakes? Who still has to learn to how to settle down? A man with a scandalous reputation?' He lifted her palm to his lips. 'A man who has occasional nightmares about the past?'

'I could.' She looked so solemn, as if making a vow. 'If you're *sure*?'

The doubt in her eyes made him vow to prove to her, daily, how much she meant to him. 'Never more so, my love.'

'A scandalous reputation sounds intriguing.' Her expression grew tender. 'And as for nightmares…they'll pass with time and help.'

She leaned up on tiptoe, her mouth brushing his in the lightest of kisses.

'I love you, Alaric. I fell for you the night we met. I still can't believe—'

He slanted his mouth over hers, relief and triumph and love overwhelming him.

She was his! He'd silence the last of her doubts. He'd devote his life to making her happy.

Much later, when the flare of passion threatened to roar out of control, Alaric stepped away.

'What are you doing? Alaric! Your leg!'

Ignoring the pain he finally managed to settle on his good knee. He held her hand tight in his, their fingers threaded together.

'I'm proposing. I want to do this right.'

'Oh.'

She looked stunned. He'd finally found a way to silence her. But she confounded him by dropping to the floor in front of him.

'Yes,' she said, her voice breathless.

'I haven't asked you yet.' He couldn't prevent the grin that split his face. Joy welled in an unstoppable flood.

'I'm saving time. You have to get off that knee.'

'In that case…' He pulled her off balance as he toppled back onto the thick carpet. She sprawled over him and his unruly body stirred.

'Alaric!' Tamsin gasped as he pulled her down hard over his groin. 'We can't. We shouldn't. You're just out of hospital!'

'We can. We will.' He kissed her soft lips and sighed his pleasure. 'You can spend your life reforming me.'

'Never. I love you just the way you are.'

She kissed him and Alaric silently gave thanks. In Tamsin he'd found the one perfect woman to make his life complete. He'd found love.

EPILOGUE

THE Gothic cathedral glowed as afternoon sunlight poured through the stained-glass windows. The scent of candles mingled with expensive perfumes and the fragrance of fresh flowers that were massed everywhere.

It was like a dream, walking down the aisle, the focus of every look. The place was crowded. Aristocracy from all around Europe, diplomats and community leaders, plus members of the public who'd been lucky enough to win a ballot to attend. But among them Tamsin spotted familiar faces: her colleagues, friends from the youth centre, Alaric's old comrades, smiling as they nodded encouragingly. Even her parents, looking proud and slightly bewildered.

But she'd barely been able to tear her gaze from the man who watched her every step with an intensity that sent heat and excitement spiralling through her.

Alaric. Tall, proud and handsome in his uniform.

His cousin Raul had stood beside him, stunningly good looking with his killer smile and black as night hair. Yet Tamsin had barely spared him a glance, her whole being focused on the man she was to marry.

Seeing the love in Alaric's eyes had made it all real as nothing else had. The luxuriously embroidered crimson velvet gown and its long train had felt unfamiliar and daunting as it trailed impressively behind her. The weight of the delicate beaten gold diadem had made her nervous, as had the filigree collar of gold and rubies circling her throat.

When she'd entered the cathedral to the triumphant blare of trumpets and swelling organ music she'd felt like an impostor, a little girl pretending to be a princess.

But from the moment Alaric's gaze had locked with hers joy had sung in her heart and the world had righted itself.

This was so right she almost cried with happiness.

Now, with the ceremony over, they faced the congregation. Alaric stood behind her and in defiance of all protocol wrapped his arms around her, pulling her close.

'Tamsin?' Pleasure skated through her at the intimate purr of his voice saying her name.

'Yes?' She struggled to focus on the smiling throng and not Alaric's hot breath feathering her neck.

'No regrets?'

'Never!' She twisted round in his arms to see his indigo eyes dark with love. Neither heard the jubilant roar of the crowd as she kissed him full on the mouth and he responded emphatically.

Afterwards everyone present attested Prince Alaric and his bride had broken tradition and married for love.

Coming Next Month

from **Harlequin Presents® EXTRA.** Available February 8, 2011.

Coming Next Month

from **Harlequin Presents®.** Available February 22, 2011.

REQUEST YOUR FREE BOOKS!

2 FREE NOVELS PLUS
2 FREE GIFTS!

YES! Please send me 2 FREE Harlequin Presents® novels and my 2 FREE gifts (gifts are worth about $10). After receiving them, if I don't wish to receive any more books, I can return the shipping statement marked "cancel." If I don't cancel, I will receive 6 brand-new novels every month and be billed just $4.05 per book in the U.S. or $4.74 per book in Canada. That's a saving of at least 15% off the cover price! It's quite a bargain! Shipping and handling is just 50¢ per book.* I understand that accepting the 2 free books and gifts places me under no obligation to buy anything. I can always return a shipment and cancel at any time. Even if I never buy another book, the two free books and gifts are mine to keep forever.

106/306 HDN E5M4

Name _____ (PLEASE PRINT) _____

Address _____ Apt. # _____

City _____ State/Prov. _____ Zip/Postal Code _____

Signature (if under 18, a parent or guardian must sign)

Mail to the **Harlequin Reader Service:**
IN U.S.A.: P.O. Box 1867, Buffalo, NY 14240-1867
IN CANADA: P.O. Box 609, Fort Erie, Ontario L2A 5X3

Not valid for current subscribers to Harlequin Presents books.

Are you a current subscriber to Harlequin Presents books and want to receive the larger-print edition? Call 1-800-873-8635 today!

* Terms and prices subject to change without notice. Prices do not include applicable taxes. N.Y. residents add applicable sales tax. Canadian residents will be charged applicable provincial taxes and GST. Offer not valid in Quebec. This offer is limited to one order per household. All orders subject to approval. Credit or debit balances in a customer's account(s) may be offset by any other outstanding balance owed by or to the customer. Please allow 4 to 6 weeks for delivery. Offer available while quantities last.

HPI0R

USA TODAY *bestselling author Lynne Graham*
is back with a thrilling new trilogy
SECRETLY PREGNANT, CONVENIENTLY WED

Three heroines must marry alpha males to keep
their dreams…but Alejandro, Angelo and Cesario
are not about to be tamed!

Book 1—JEMIMA'S SECRET
Available March 2011 from Harlequin Presents®.

JEMIMA yanked open a drawer in the sideboard to find Alfie's birth certificate. Her son was her husband's child. It was a question of telling the truth whether she liked it or not. She extended the certificate to Alejandro.

"This has to be nonsense," Alejandro asserted.

"Well, if you can find some other way of explaining how I managed to give birth by that date and Alfie not be yours, I'd like to hear it," Jemima challenged.

Alejandro glanced up, golden eyes bright as blades and as dangerous. "All this proves is that you must still have been pregnant when you walked out on our marriage. It does not automatically follow that the child is mine."

"'I know it doesn't suit you to hear this news now and I really didn't want to tell you. But I can't lie to you about it. Someday Alfie may want to look you up and get acquainted."

"If what you have just told me is the truth, if that little boy does prove to be mine, it was vindictive and extremely selfish of you to leave me in ignorance!"

Jemima paled. "When I left you, I had no idea that I was still pregnant."

"Two years is a long period of time, yet you made no attempt to inform me that I might be a father. I will want DNA tests to confirm your claim before I make any decision about what I want to do."

"Do as you like," she told him curtly. "*I* know who Alfie's father is and there has never been any doubt of his identity."

"I will make arrangements for the tests to be carried out and I will see you again when the result is available," Alejandro drawled with lashings of dark Spanish masculine reserve.

"I'll contact a solicitor and start the divorce," Jemima proffered in turn.

Alejandro's eyes narrowed in a piercing scrutiny that made her uncomfortable. "It would be foolish to do anything before we have that DNA result."

"I disagree," Jemima flashed back. "I should have applied for a divorce the minute I left you!"

Alejandro quirked an ebony brow. "And why didn't you?"

Jemima dealt him a fulminating glance but said nothing, merely moving past him to open her front door in a blunt invitation for him to leave.

"I'll be in touch," he delivered on the doorstep.

What is Alejandro's next move? Perhaps rekindling their marriage is the only solution! But will Jemima agree?

*Find out in Lynne Graham's
exciting new romance
JEMIMA'S SECRET*

*Available March 2011
from Harlequin Presents®.*

Start your Best Body today with these top 3 nutrition tips!

1. **SHOP THE PERIMETER OF THE GROCERY STORE:** The good stuff—fruits, veggies, lean proteins and dairy—always line the outer edges of the store. When you veer into the center aisles, you enter the temptation zone, where the unhealthy foods live.

2. **WATCH PORTION SIZES:** Most portion sizes in restaurants are nearly twice the size of a true serving and at home, it's easy to "clean your plate." Use these easy serving guidelines:
   - Protein: the palm of your hand
   - Grains or Fruit: a cup of your hand
   - Veggies: the palm of two open hands

3. **USE THE RAINBOW RULE FOR PRODUCE:** Your produce drawers should be filled with every color of fruits and vegetables. The greater the variety, the more vitamins and other nutrients you add to your diet.

Find these and many more helpful tips in

YOUR BEST BODY NOW

by

TOSCA RENO

WITH STACY BAKER

Bestselling Author of
THE EAT-CLEAN DIET®

YOUR BEST BODY NOW

Look and Feel Fabulous at Any Age the Eat-Clean Way

☑ Get Toned with the Energy-Boosting Muscle Makeover
☑ Look 10 Years Younger with Tosca's Beauty Clock-Stoppers
☑ Blast Belly Fat with 50 All-New Recipes

TOSCA RENO

Available wherever books are sold!

HARLEQUIN *Presents*

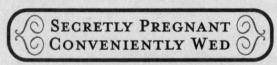